WITHDRAWN

withdrawn

TORTALL

A SPY'S GUIDE

Tortall Books
by Tamora Pierce

TORTALL

A SPY'S GUIDE

TAMORA PIERCE

WITH JULIE HOLDERMAN, TIMOTHY LIEBE,
AND MEGAN MESSINGER

ILLUSTRATIONS BY EVA WIDERMANN

RANDOM HOUSE 🏠 NEW YORK

This is a work of fiction. Names, characters, places, and incidents either are the product of the author's imagination or are used fictitiously. Any resemblance to actual persons, living or dead, events, or locales is entirely coincidental.

Text copyright © 2017 by Tamora Pierce LLC
Cover art copyright © 2017 by Velvet Spectrum
Interior illustrations copyright © 2017 by Eva Widermann
Map copyright © 2017 by Isidre Mones

All rights reserved. Published in the United States by Random House Children's Books,
a division of Penguin Random House LLC, New York.

Random House and the colophon are registered trademarks of Penguin Random House LLC.

Visit us on the Web! randomhouseteens.com
Educators and librarians, for a variety of teaching tools, visit us at RHTeachersLibrarians.com

Library of Congress Cataloging-in-Publication Data is available upon request.

ISBN 978-0-375-86767-5 (trade) — ISBN 978-0-375-96767-2 (lib. bdg.)
ISBN 978-0-375-89849-5 (ebook)

MANUFACTURED IN CHINA
10 9 8 7 6 5 4 3 2 1
First Edition

Random House Children's Books supports the First Amendment
and celebrates the right to read.

*To Julie, Tim, Megan, Lisa, Judy Gerjuoy (reading
this from the Summerlands), Chelsea, Mallory, and
the residents of Tortall and its neighbors: my
heartfelt thanks and devotion eternal*
—T.P.

*To Tammy, who gave me the opportunity; my fellow
writers, who gave me the ride of my life; and my
parents, Steve and Evelyn, who taught me
I could do whatever I wanted as long as
I was willing to work for it*
—J.H.

*To Tamora Pierce, who always asks "Are you writing?"
And in memory of Judy Gerjuoy*
—T.L.

*For Mom and Dad, my first and best reading buddies;
Joey, my favorite brother (and not just because it's only
the two of us!); and, most of all, everything here is for
you, Tammy—there are not words for how
you have lifted me up*
—M.M.

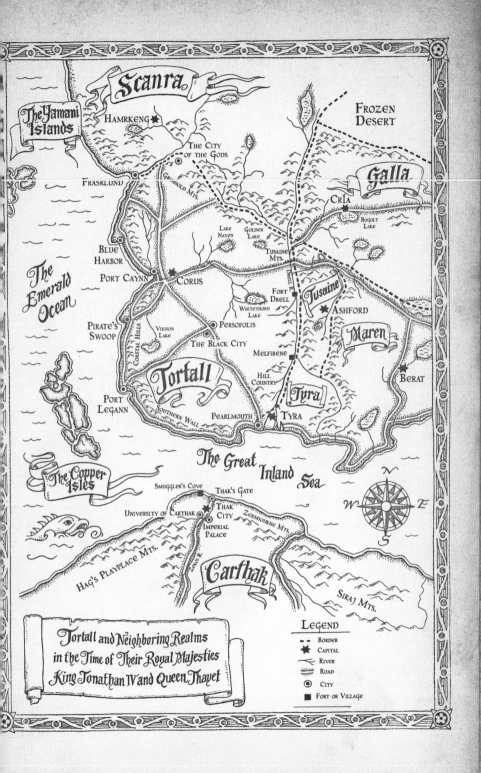

Tortall and Neighboring Realms
in the Time of Their Royal Majesties
King Jonathan IV and Queen Thayet

LEGEND

- - - BORDER
★ CAPITAL
~ RIVER
ROAD
◉ CITY
■ FORT OR VILLAGE

Greetings, old friends and newcomers to the backstreets of the Tortall universe! As the author of eighteen books and quite a few short stories set in the fantasy realm of Tortall and its neighbors, I have been working in this setting since 1976. Fans and friends have often mentioned how much more I know about the universe than I include in my published work. With that in mind, some friends and I have pulled together a Tortallan spy's guide and a mass of notes, as well as bits and pieces of daily life. With the assistance of the editors and artists at Random House Children's Books, we offer you one of the realm's most useful inside views. It provides a *very* behind-the-scenes look at Tortall's inner workings, in addition to a much-demanded timeline. I hope you have as much fun reading this as we did creating it!

So here is *Tortall: A Spy's Guide,* the contents of a crate that spymaster George Cooper began sorting through on the day he realized he needed the room beside his office for . . . well, you'll see soon enough. It's a never-before-seen look at profiles of people of interest, letters alerting the spymasters to strange goings-on, correspondence, teaching materials, and family papers.

With my goodwill and that of my companions,

Tamora Pierce

Letters from the Cooper
Family Archives

Coded for the eyes of the Whisper Man ONLY
October 14, 466 H.E.
From the Sign of the Sheaves, Arenaver

Dearest George,

Do you remember that time we had together
in Blue Harbor back in May? You said we carried
on like youngsters. I told you in April I'd fought
a mage who guarded a smuggler's crew. He lobbed
some manner of sticky magic at me. It got under my
armor—you saw the burns on my neck and chest. My
ember-stone seemed undamaged, as was that other,
<u>special</u> charm I wear, remember? The one I said I
should just give up with my Change of Life dancing
around me, but we both knew I jested? Then after
that battle, as we were shipping the smugglers off
to justice, a storm blew up and I forgot the whole
thing. I hied myself off to Blue Harbor and you
once I got the chance.

Right now you are frowning and telling me
to stop fluttering and spit out the crab that has got
hold of my tongue.

I'm pregnant, laddybuck. When I started
puking, I looked up Neal, who serves as healer

1

for Lady Kel at New Haven. (She and Neal send greetings to you.) Neal said I might do as I please with my charm, for it was useless for preventing a pregnancy. That mage had stripped its spell. My ember-stone is unchanged—nothing can touch the Goddess's power. So now I wear my no-fertility charm in that second right-ear piercing you don't like. I think it makes me look piratical. Now pregnantly piratical.

I bade farewell to the north. In two days, I will be in Corus. There I have arranged an audience with Their Majesties, where I mean to offer my resignation as King's Champion.

Dearest, I am serious this time. When I said I was thinking about it back in May, you laughed, but I was telling the truth. On damp days I need winches in my shoulders so I can get a sword over my head. I love the modified jousting saddle that you had made for me, as it braces my hips and lower back for a long day of riding. But truth to tell, my work needs someone who doesn't creak so much.

Now the Goddess gives me as clear a sign as a woman could want. It is time for me to place my sword before Jonathan and Thayet and tell them to find a new Champion. I have no replacement to recommend, but I am sure the king has been turning possibilities over in his mind for the past decade. Also, I am sure Her Majesty will not object to a change. She's been <u>hinting</u> that I need to retire. Kindly, of course, but she has noticed my winces.

Whoever my replacement is, I wish him well. I know it will be a "him," but there's naught I can do about that. Lady Kel has made it clear that she is too sane for the work that I have done, and the more recent girls have yet to obtain their shields.

Once that is over, I will come home to my patient, forbearing lover and have our child. And this time I mean to <u>stay</u> home. I won't do as I did with the twins and Thom, leaving them to you and our servants to raise. I mean to help with this one. (The midwife promises it's <u>only</u> one this time.) That's fair. It was my carelessness in not examining my charm that has presented us with this newest token of the Goddess's favor.

I do not know how long Their Majesties intend to keep me in the capital. Not very long, I think. And then I will make my way to you somehow. I would like to say I will ride, but the way things are going, I believe any healers I talk to will order me to take ship to the Swoop. Pray for good weather, I beg. It is so unromantic to come home while puking over the rail.

I would apologize for the new token of our affection, but I remember how you always teased that you would be happy for more children. I also remember that when you tease you often speak the truth. So here I come, my belly leading the way, to fulfill your wish just a little.

With all my love,
and a new hatchling in my nest,

Alanna

November 20, 466 H.E.

decoded

To Thom of Trebond
   School of Mages
   The Royal University
   Corus, Tortall

From George Cooper, Baron
      Pirate's Swoop
      Tortall

Dear Thom,

   I am glad to read that you will be coming home for
Midwinter Festival. It will cheer your mother, who is
already starting to show her condition. I've also invited your
grandfather and grandmother to stay, so we shall manage
to amuse ourselves pretty well, I think.

   In fact, since they are coming, why don't you ride
with them? They will be journeying with other travelers
through the Royal Forest, but I know they will enjoy your
company, and you will be safer. You would also be doing
your parents a favor if you would buy a pound or two
of orange and anise tea, which your mother is drinking
by the bucket, and candied oranges and limes, which she
yearns for and we cannot get. Ask your grandfather for

sufficient coin and tell him I will repay him when I see him. Buy yourself a good meal or two while you are about it.

Do you remember the room next to my office? The one where you children stayed when you were small, so I could mind you while your nurse helped about the fief? You told me it was a danger of fire with all the crates of old papers I stored in there once you three got too big for it. I think that your ma's vow to stay home with this baby will last as long as winter, and I'll need the old room again. I've been cleaning it out and reading some of what's in those crates. Strange to find so many reminders of how it was in those first days, when Their Majesties were deciding how they should rule and your grandfather Myles, John Juggler, and I were thrashing out the beginnings of the Shadow Service.

Should I save the lessons you boys and your sister wrote, to show your children one day?

Your mother and I look forward to seeing you and hearing about your studies. Remember to wrap up well on your way through the forest. The winter there is a harsh one.

Your loving father,

George

Becoming a Spy

Marked for Fast Passage
To the Whisper Man

decoded

September 21, 448

To the Whisper Man

From Evin Larse / Callum Larse

The village of Dowling Falls,
near Fief Sinthya

Sir,

Forgive me for stealing my dad's spy device, but I've
been writing code for him to send you since I was ten, so I
knew that much of your business already. The thing is, I
think there's a problem here, and Da says I have too much
imagination, even though he's the one that taught me a
Player can't have too much imagination.

Company Larse & Quill has been playing the
Whitethorn Valley all summer. Mostly business is good,
and there's been plenty of coin in the cap, if not so much
tasty news to send along to you.

Presently we're settled here in Dowling Falls. It
serves two good-sized temples, a big market, and it's a
crossroads to the fiefdoms of Sinthya, Nond, Fickle Lynn,
and Ketan, as well as the Great Roads East and West.

There's something going on at Sinthya. More

merchants' wagons take the road there than to any of the other fiefs. (My da says they could be bound for Ketan or Fickle Lynn, but I follow as many of them as I can, and they all go through Sinthya's gate.) And when the road is muddy these wagons sink deep. I was curious and had a look. The baskets hide locked wooden boxes. Some of them are magicked, too.

Men are taking the road to Sinthya as well, with the wagons or on horseback. They're hard types who drink little, keep to themselves, and ride armed. Some wear chain vests or leather jerkins with metal rings sewn to them. Almost all of them have sword or knife scars.

Da says I make a whole loaf from pigeon crumbs. I think Sinthya plots war with his neighbors, or rebellion.

Tell me what I must do, please.

Evin Larse

1) Put in a word with Thayet and Sarge to have a spot kept open for Evin Larse in next year's recruit class for the Queen's Riders. See how the lad does with them.
2) Write young Evin and tell him to continue to report on events at Fief Sinthya.
3) Write Callum Larse and ask him to remain in the area for the winter, keeping eyes and ears open. Send him a decent-sized purse so he and his people don't lose by it.
4) Have our Nursemaid in Dowling Falls bribe both temples to have the Players perform over the winter holidays.
5) Advise the army to have troops ready to move in the spring.

A Workbook for a Young Spy

>)•●•((

For my dearest daughter, Aly, here is
the answer to all those questions you've been
asking! Now that you are entering my service,
you must learn to obey me as your chief. Only
ask spying questions when no one else will
hear, just as you swore in your oath to me.

—Da, the Whisper Man

>)•●•((

A warrior walks so everyone knows she is there.
No one knows the spy is there.
A warrior seems to do everything.
A spy seems to do nothing.
A warrior fights whenever she can.
A spy fights only as a last resort.
A warrior wins fame.
A spy who wins fame is dead.

Appearance

Disguises are overrated. They encourage a spy to skulk, which draws attention. Folk notice a person who tries to be sneaky. Walk and act like you belong.

Changing your walk or the way you stand is often a better disguise than a wig and an eye patch. Put something in your shoe, like a pebble. Yes, it will hurt. It will also give you a limp and make you favor that foot as you stand. It will change your entire shape. Folk might look at you and say, "Well, she resembles that lass or that lad, but it's not her." A pebble in the mouth changes the shape of the cheek in the same way. Remember how it feels to have an aching tooth. Favor that side. Keep a hand to it, or a scarf. That will redden your face. Folk will think you're someone else. Put snarls and dirt or grease in your hair. Be sure your nails are dirty. Grime in your teeth, or black wax, is helpful. Smear dirt or soot on face and hands. Grab a basket or armful of folded laundry, or a bottle of polish and smelly rags, and you become nearly invisible.

A servant's clothes or the clothes of someone desperately poor are the best disguises in most places. Folk don't like to look at the truly poor, and servants are for ordering about. If you're clothed cheap, put on cheap shoes or take yours off. In such disguises, answer all those better dressed than you as "sir" or "my lord" or "mistress" or "my lady" and look at the ground. Those that have no coin don't meet the eyes of those as do. Don't talk. Take orders even if those giving them have no right to give them, and scuttle off right quick. Never argue. The robes of novices are good disguises for the same reason—folk only see the robe—but I don't like them. The first priestess you encounter will want to know your temple and she'll quiz you on the rites. You will be wanted to do the things your order requires, and others of that order will know you aren't truly one of theirs. It's too risky. Also, there's the chance the god will take offense.

Poor folk and servants don't walk the center of the way like they own it. They walk to the sides. They slouch unless they are upper servants, who imitate their masters. Practice your slouch with a milkmaid's yoke on your shoulders, or the yoke used by stable lads and kitchen servants as they fetch water. Fetch milk and water while you are at it. Practice is good for you.

Remember, do not <u>wear</u> a disguise. <u>Be</u> it. You are not dressed up as a Player. You <u>are</u> a Player. You live three-quarters of the year on the road, bathe in streams, go barefoot, pass the hat, mend costumes, and do what your elders tell you. Know the names of your family, the company you travel with, and the towns and fiefdoms you've performed at. Speak with Evin Larse and the Players who visit us. If your disguise is that of a one-eyed fisher girl seeking work in a small village, think yourself into believing you see naught with that eye. Busy yourself with boning fish and mending nets. Let the folk in our own fishing village teach you how it's done. Memorize the kinds of fish, the folk of the village, the headman's name, and

the names of the lord and his family. If you've a story—
you're a runaway, a farmer, a palace maid, you're from Blue
Harbor—make sure it's a whole one, with all the details
close to hand. It's the difference between a successful
lie and getting caught. Make as much of it the truth as
possible. That way there's less for you to remember. Know
it all like it's yours, for your very life may depend on it.

A beggar's disguise is best for all-around
usefulness. Except for the richest neighborhoods, beggars
go everywhere. Even in the richest places they can be seen
at the rear gates. A bit of damp bread mashed with honey
set like boils on the face, legs, and arms to draw flies, as
well as filthy rags, a battered crutch and a bandaged leg
(also good to hide an extra blade, or a silver coin or two for

bribes), a bowl or cup, and you
can wander and sit anywhere
without anyone to look at you
twice. (The nastier the boils,
the less they'll look, even as
they toss a coin in your bowl.)
You'll have to pay the Rogue's
chief for the area where you set
up, and be sure to give half
your earnings to Somal, the
beggar's god, for the families
of them that are truly hurt.
Somal is kind as long as real
beggars benefit.

At night no one in the cheap drinking houses will blink if you put down a coin for a bowl of soup or pay a lad to fetch you one from a better food seller. While you nurse your meal, all around you will talk. So will those who see you every day. Shopkeepers and their folk are often glad of a listening ear. Servants wanting a rest will ask for the day's news. Ask the right questions of such folk and you have informants soon enough.

Talk and Informants

Know the accent and the words that go with your disguise. If your guise comes from Frasrlund, don't talk as if you come from Port Caynn. The two don't sound the same. Don't claim to be a Bazhir if you can't speak their tongue well.

Best of all, talk as little as you can. Being in the Shadow Service of spies, you know all manner of secret things. You can't get in trouble when you hold your tongue. Good listeners live longer and learn a great deal. True, it's <u>hard</u> to keep quiet when you know more than the folk you're with! Keep quiet anyway.

No one expects a woman busy at her chores to pay attention to what's being said around her. Never mind if a man's mother and sisters show they heard everything while they stitched or kneaded. He'll still think a woman saves all her thought for work. You're a far better spy mopping the floor than clanking with daggers.

In Carthak and the west beyond Maren, there is no

better informant than a slave. No one notices them. They may go anywhere and look into anything if they are careful. Disguised as a slave, you may ask questions that would be suspicious coming from others. Everyone believes a slave is stupid, even given evidence he is not.

At court, listen to how folk talk to Their Majesties and to each other. Nobles shower royalty with compliments, asking after the princes and princesses and praising Their Majesties on the fine work they do for the kingdom. Then listen to the way your quarry speaks of Their Majesties to their friends. I will wager you a month's allowance that they do not speak of Their Majesties and Their Highnesses in nearly the same way as when they are facing them.

This is true of most folk who want to keep their positions, and their heads. We listen to servants and to nobles alike. Then we decide what is simply malice and what is danger to the realm.

Folk will always try to make themselves look wise or clever to a newcomer or a pretty girl. They will pretend to be important by giving away secrets if a spy asks the right questions. Rascals will tell you all manner of fine things to get you to give them kisses and more. There's many a fellow who will try to bed a lass who appears interested as she gets him to talk. And mind yourself carefully, as any woman spy must. The least of us can make a slip of our own in the arms of a lover. Best not to take one.

There will be times when you will hear things that you don't like. Things offensive to Their Majesties, who are your godsparents, to your ma or da, or to your friends. Ignore the offense if you wish to enter the Shadow Service. Should you ever give away to strangers that you've been eavesdropping, I shall be forced to drop you from my roll of young spies. A good one <u>never</u> shows that she's heard anything. Talk it over with me, if you like. I'm your spymaster, after all. But you can't be losing your temper over what you hear, or you'll never be good at this.

Suspicious Folk

You have the Sight. It shows you when someone is lying, but don't rely on it. Learn the signs of a liar. Does that person blink or look away as he talks? He's lying. Even folk who don't know what they're looking at sense it when people are being dodgy. The twitch at the corner of the mouth and a look-away glance serve as alarm bells. That's why it's important for <u>you</u> to meet someone's gaze, unless you play the servant and need to look down.

Another giveaway is too many protests that the speaker is dishing out the truth. The saying "the truth speaks for itself" means just that. Folk who tell the truth don't think they must keep repeating it. It's the truth—it's obvious. Only liars tell it over and over, trying to hammer their lie into others' minds.

I'll say it until your ears turn blue. Silence is better than talk. If you don't listen, you can't hear the little breaks in the voice that could mean a lie, a sorrow, or something left out. If you don't listen, you won't hear those few words from the quiet folk who know more than all the braggarts.

If someone joins your group who's jolly and friendly, always has coin to buy others food or a drink, or friends who can find just the right weapon, spell, or horse in a pinch? The kind of lad or lass that you just want to trust and confide your secrets to? Get rid of him. Like as not, that's the one hired by your enemies. That one will get inside your group and turn you all in to the magistrate once they've gathered—or planted—enough evidence to put a noose around your necks.

If you're asked to join a conspiracy that's run by someone like this? Run. That conspiracy is set up by a spymaster to be used against his enemies, sometimes to build a conspiracy where none existed before. To prove a king has enemies in order that his magistrates may lay down harsh laws or put a popular noble's head on the chopping block. False conspiracies can be used to justify higher taxes and civil wars.

And again, keep your eye on those quiet ones who are overlooked by the rest. They see more than they tell, and they think more than they talk. You want them for your friends, in case they've noticed something you haven't. You don't want them asking questions about you.

Danger—Magic

Essence spells are the main things we spies must worry about. We carry our essences everywhere, in our skin, hair, and nails. All we touch picks up some of our essence. The longer we touch things, the more essence we place on them. This is also true if our feelings are on the boil, if we're ill, or if we're hurt—anything that makes us sweat. This is why spies and Provost's Guards alike value things like clothing someone has worn. Mages can use that clothing to draw the essence out and work a spell. Wear the silk gloves and stockings I gave you—they will hold your essence inside them. If you don't have them about you, pick items up with a bit of cloth. Leave nothing behind. If you can't take something with your essence on it, burn the thing or sink it in deep water. That will carry your essence away. Luckily essence mages are rare, but there's no use in taking chances.

Magic draws magic. Wear no charms or amulets unless they've been given to you by a god. If that happens, mages will notice you have it and try to find you by tracking it, but it's to be hoped the god will help look after you.

Sneaking

Before you enter a room, look at the doorsill (or windowsills if you go that way). Suspicious folk often place a line of chalk or flour where someone might step or place a hand, to reveal that someone has entered the room. Do not disturb it. Check the doorframe for hairs placed across the crack or splinters of wood stuck inside it. (Canny folk who know the game may use two or three splinters of wood.) Put these things back <u>just where you found them</u> when you leave. Use them in your own rooms, on door- and windowsills. Such precautions can gain a spy hours' or days' worth of time to escape pursuers.

Check also for places to hide. Look behind curtains and tapestries for nooks, window embrasures, and balconies. Don't hide beneath a desk. Oftentimes when folk come into a room, one of them will sit there. Find a second way out, and a third. If you have no rope and might need to leave through a window, see if you can readily cut or tear curtains or tapestries to provide yourself with one. Remember the servants' stair in a castle, a costly house, or an expensive inn. Remember the city's rooftops. Southern cities, with their flat roofs, are a spy's dream. Remember castle privies, which empty into the moats. The smell is not so pleasant, nor the feel, but better that than torture and death.

In a chase, always keep in mind, <u>folk seldom look up.</u> You are better off in a tree or on a roof than in a shed or behind a woodpile. Fools say that if you run up or down the waters of a stream, hounds cannot track you. This is claptrap. Hounds, particularly good ones, can catch your scent above water. You're better off on stone or finding a river or lake you can swim. If you're in a thick wood, get into the boughs and go from tree to tree. Scent rises, a mage once told me. A hound may track you to a tree, but if you are ten or twenty trees away, he cannot follow.

Stop as soon as you are able and <u>wait.</u> Your pursuers may return to where they lost you to cast about again.

Many a runaway has been caught when he came down from his tree too soon.

Speaking of hounds, if you enter the grounds of house or temple, bring a treat for them. If you like dogs, and I know you do, dose your treat with a sleep potion instead of poison. Most shops that sell to dog owners carry potions to keep a dog in slumber when his thrashing might put a wound or broken bone in danger. If you work with one who dislikes dogs, remind him there's more than one god that likes them and will take it poorly if he uses poison. Worse, at least in Tortall, there's the Wildmage. She's not as reasonable as most gods.

Stay clear of chickens and geese. Both are noisy and, as you know all too well, geese will attack. Think how red your face will be when you must tell your spymaster you were driven off by geese.

Wear dark clothes and soft shoes when you search a sleeping house. Darken your skin. Step on stone or rugs where you can. Take care at each joining of corridors to listen for movement. Retreat before you go ahead if you are in doubt. Remember a spy's first task, to go unseen and unheard.

Protecting Yourself

Get in the habit of making your room secure, preparing it for your safety. Arrange your weapons so that they are between you and the windows and the doors. Start with blades beneath your pillow and your bed. Don't forget to add any weapons that came with the room. If there are weapons on the walls, make sure right off if you can pull them from the walls and out of any sheaths they may have. Even if it's dull as ditch water, a blade can be used as a club.

Be sure you can reach all of your weapons easily in the dark. When traveling, try to get a room that grants escape through a window. To make a room safer, move any heavy furniture to block the door, even if you must use your bed. Pile things before the window so any who enter there will make enough noise to wake you.

If you are offered a room with no window, consider sleeping in the stables. If your mask is that of a beggar, stable or barn is the only place you will be allowed to sleep anyway.

Never take wine or anything that will make you sleep soundly in a place that is not Pirate's Swoop.

Wherever you are, make it a habit to spot the things you can use as weapons. Indoors you have furniture, metalware, stoneware, and hangings to throw over an attacker's head. Outdoors stones are almost always at hand. On town streets, the sticks used to prop awnings can serve as staffs. If a gang comes after you, is there a cartload of vegetables or barrels you can push into its way? Herds of animals and folk on horseback are good distractions. Ropes can entangle pursuers or be used to tie them up.

In a marketplace, if you sense you are followed, find a seller of bright-polished silver or brassware, or a seller of well-polished swords and daggers. Angle the polished metal so that, in appearing to admire it, you will see what is over your shoulder reflected in the blade. Does someone eye you? Does someone too quickly pretend to be looking over a seller's goods? Did someone duck into a shop? Walk on a way and check behind you again to see if that person is still there.

To lose a follower, know that every shop, stable, eating house, guard station, temple, warehouse, and tavern has more than one door. Enter there, duck down through the crowd, and escape through the back way. Tell the muscle lads who guard the tavern, the Provost's Guards on watch, or any clutch of brave sailors that a pursuer has frightened you, and point him out. Or, if you are working, tuck yourself into a back-alley doorway with blade in hand, single out a likely-looking pursuer, let him go by just a little bit, get your arm around his neck, tickle his ribs with the blade, and ask what he means by dogging you. Do not pop out right off if you don't see him when you expect to. <u>Listen.</u> He might be breathing just on the other side of your doorframe.

If you are in a place for more than a day, I expect you to know the best spots to dodge pursuit, eye anyone suspicious, and get information on them.

Fighting

Don't ever let your poor old da hear of you trying to fight straight up with a knight, a soldier, even an ordinary tavern brawler, or I'll be forced to disown you. Fighting is not a spy's job. We listen. We read documents. We code and break code. We run. We collect and pass on information. We need to be <u>alive</u> to do that. When we fight, unless it's to escape, we betray our duty to our spymasters.

So. If you're cornered by a big muscly fellow with a grin on his face, you throw dirt, perfume, or vinegar in his eyes and you run.

Of course, it's not always so easy.

Remember the main targets on an enemy. Eye. Throat. Manhood, unless you deal with a woman. She won't like a blow there, either. If you wear boots or shoes with heels, strike the foot. The arch is best, but those tiny toes break well, too. And then, when your foe

is on his knees? Kick him down and run. It doesn't matter if you can beat him to a pulp right then or no. An injured spy—and you'll get hurt in a fight—is no good to anyone, so no fighting more than you must!

Practice running.

Other Tender Spots

Should an enemy seize you and fail to let go:

Grip a finger—any will do, but the little finger is best—and bend it back. Your captor should scream in pain and release you before you break it. If he doesn't free you, break it. He'll release you. Run.

See the pale half-moon—the Mother's Mark—at the base of most people's fingernails? Take your thumbnail (this is why mine are my thickest and strongest nails) and thrust it into your foe's Mother's Mark until your captor screams in pain and releases you. Run.

Seize your captor's hand, and bend it <u>forward</u> on his wrist as far as it will go. Grip it in that position so he cannot free himself. You can force him to his knees in this manner. Make him swear—before you cripple the arm for life—on his soul, by Mithros, not to chase you. If he breaks that oath, he'll have worse problems in this world than catching you. Run.

Seize your foe's arm. Twist it behind his back. Grip the elbow and thrust it up along his back toward his neck. This puts hard pressure on his wrist, if you still hold it, and his elbow. If you push hard, you can break the arm.

Finish as I suggest for the move above. Run.

If you are at court, the pretty Yamani fans newly come into fashion serve as weapons. Folded, they make a fine jabbing stick. There is a special Yamani fan made of razor-sharp steel, but you need special training in its use. Also, they are made only in the Yamani Islands. I think a certain young lady will have to be very good at her work if she would like her da to get her one for Midwinter!

Don't forget the pins that hold a lady's veils and hair in place, or brooch pins. They can be very discouraging to a foe. There's little room in a gown's tight-fitting sleeves for blades, though Her Majesty says that new fashions are leaning to a wider sleeve.

Your ma would be happy to teach you some of what she knows, if you were to ask. It's a different way of fighting than a spy's, but she's learned some wicked tricks in her travels. Give her a chance.

One More Thing

Gather it all, young spy,
but tell it only to your spymaster.
No one else. Secrets are power.
They're the only coin that matters,
so let us hoard ours!

decoder's note: Birdsong/
Alianne of Pirate's Swoop is but
12 years of age at this writing.

April 23, 459 H.E.

Personal report of agent apprentice Birdsong
Concerning the events of April 21, 459 H.E.
In the city of Pearlmouth, Tortall

At noon on the 21st of April, I was informed by
~~my father~~ the Whisper Man that I was to have the
chance to watch a trade of money for information in
a private room at a public house in this city. (I have
been ordered not to write down the name or the street
of the meeting place.) I put on the brown dress,
white apron, and cap of a maidservant and wore it
under a cloak. Then I followed the Whisper Man
from the inn where we lodged to the public house
at six of the clock, three hours in advance of the
meeting.

    The Whisper Man bought a room on the same
floor as the one in which our true meeting was to
take place. Once there, the Whisper Man ordered
a meal and a bottle of wine. When these things

came, he ordered the servants not to disturb us and locked our door. He then opened the window. We had already inspected the building. The outside stonework is very old, with many gaps to serve as hand- and toeholds. We used them to climb to the room where the Whisper Man was to meet his informants. The shutters were open, so we entered it easily.

There was a main room with a table, four chairs, hearth (there was no fire in the hearth, the day being mild), and a small bedchamber. The opening to the bedroom was covered by a tapestry that reached from near the ceiling to the floor. I hid myself behind it, standing back far enough that my shoes did not show.

While I waited, the Whisper Man sat at the table and wrote in his records book in code. He could hear if I fidgeted or sat to ease my aching ankles or sighed or cursed because I had to stand for so long or moved to sit on the bed. I did none of these things. I told him that I am ready to go into the field and I <u>swore</u> I was going to prove I was right. My biggest dream is to be a field agent! Instead of fussing, I relaxed and let my mind rest, even though my ankles and knees did ache quite fiercely.

The clock struck nine, the hour for the meet, yet the agent code-named Rushpipe did not come. I began to think wickedly of various tortures from my books that I might use on him in the name of my ankles. At last I heard the innkeeper's keys, and then the opening of the door.

"I have not seen another man, sir," I heard the innkeeper say. He must have been talking to someone else. No one calls the Whisper Man "sir" unless he wears his noble's gear. "I am sure he will be—you! This is not your room!"

"You must forgive my little trick in changing," the Whisper Man said. "I am a cautious fellow."

"It is well enough, innkeeper." That was a stranger's voice. I supposed it belonged to Rushpipe. "Leave us." I heard the clink of coins and the sound of footsteps. The noises were confusing. I soon learned it was because while I heard the innkeeper go, Rushpipe had come into the room with two other fellows.

The Whisper Man said, "Rushpipe, our business is private. Send those two away."

Rushpipe answered, "I trust my friends."

The Whisper Man said, "I do not. They may leave."

Rushpipe replied, "They are coming with us—it will do you no good to struggle!"

The Whisper Man did not cry out, but he did not have to. I heard the bang as his chair fell over. I thrust my hands through the slits in my skirt seams and drew my daggers as I peered out from behind the tapestry. My The Whisper Man struggled with two big men while a third watched. The backs of all three strangers were to me.

I came out of the tapestry right behind the closest man and stabbed him in the kidneys as I had been taught. When he went down, one of the big fellows released the Whisper Man and turned on me. He had a set of shackles in his hand that he plainly meant to use on the Whisper Man. As he turned, my companion kicked his feet from under him. The shackle-bearer fell straight into the fireless hearth so hard that he cracked his head on the stones. He did not move.

The third man hurled a knife at me. I dropped to the ground and rolled under the table. I cut his hamstrings, but the Whisper Man also did something to him that I didn't see. That was what finished him off.

We left by climbing down the outside of the

public house, keeping to the shadows. We returned to the inn where we had been staying. There we gathered our belongings and horses. Disguised as a merchant and his son, we crossed the town by way of backstreets to one of the Whisper Man's safe houses.

April 23,

There, Da! Is that a good report? All it needs is proper coding. I thought you wouldn't want me putting in how we hugged each other and all.

Aly

By the hand and personal cypher
of Baron Sir Myles of Olau
To the Whisper Man

George,

One of my frequent correspondents from
Pearlmouth wrote to me of a peculiar event
that took place at his establishment on
April 23: the killing of three men of Tusaine,
apparently by a merchant of some kind. The
merchant appears to have vanished. So too
has his companion, a maidservant in her early
teens.

His descriptions of man and girl were
very thorough. Truly, George, can you do
nothing with your nose? It is unmistakable
in combination with your eyes. The girl, of
course, is equally identifiable to one who
knows her well.

What wicked god possessed you to take my
only granddaughter into that situation? Even
if she were not actually present when trouble
broke out, what would she have done had you
been captured or killed?

I know that you say she has a talent for our

work, but she has not been raised in the streets as you were. To risk her well-being in a venture such as the one my innkeeper friend described to me, with three men left dead in a pool of blood . . .

I am <u>deeply</u> distressed, George. I tremble to think what either of our wives would do if they knew of it! Certainly I shall not be daft enough to tell them. I demand that you cease to risk Aly in fieldwork <u>at once</u> as the price for my silence. Truly, I am furious that you showed such an appalling lack of judgment.

Myles

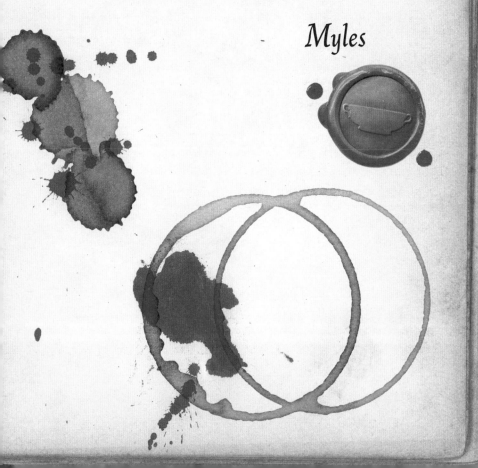

By the hand and personal cypher
of the Whisper Man
To Baron Sir Myles of Olau

Myles, forgive me.

Indeed, you've said naught to me that I have
not already said to myself. I deserved what you say
and more. My only explanation—it's no excuse, for
there is none—is that I am so giddy with my girl's
skills at the Great Work that I lost my head. I shall
not do so again. She does not know it yet, but I mean
to keep her at coding and decoding correspondence
from here on out. It is a waste, but better a waste of
her talent than her precious life.

I swear, I had <u>no</u> reason to think Rushpipe had
turned when I brought Aly to that cursed meeting.
He was a steady source of good information for
over ten years for me as thief and spy. I've had him
checked, double-checked, and approved by John
Juggler's Falcons every two years, according to
agreed-upon procedure.

Before you suggest it, I already told John
Juggler to upend the Tusaine organization and
inspect everyone in it from top to toe due to this. If

my girl hadn't been there, I would have said it was a stroke of luck that gave away the rot in that setup. Of course, if she hadn't been there, like as not I would be dead. They caught me cold, Myles. She saved my life.

Be that as it may, I have been burning frankincense to Mithros, the Goddess, and Trickster that our wives never learn of this.

Your rueful son-in-law,

George

Written in a shifting-character code developed by
Numair Salmalín, from Sir Myles's office at the
Chancellory of Information in the palace at Corus, to
Baron George Cooper's residence at Pirate's Swoop

Day After Awakening, 466 H.E.

To my lord Baron George of Pirate's Swoop
From Baron Myles of Barony Olau

With regard to Evin Larse's Overview to
the Royal Tortallan Shadow Service Guide

My dear George,

I have just read Evin's initial writing of the
Overview, and I have some concerns. Do you
not think Evin's approach is rather slapdash?
Surely he ought to take a more serious
approach to a business in which people easily
lose their lives.

Please don't misunderstand me. I like Evin.
I trust him implicitly as our Chief Falcon.
His style of operation works very well for
those field Agents you've taken to calling
Hostlers. I admit, reluctantly, that he gives
them the "dash" it needs to appeal to the kind
of superior—and chance-taking—talent in

our ranks. A sharper Shadow Service will enable us to pull ahead of the very excellent Tyran, Marenite, and Yamani services. Until we improve the quality of our own Agents, we will continue to be the recipients of nasty surprises like the recent Carthaki invasions.

However, <u>must</u> he be so casual? Ours is a serious business, something Evin knows perfectly well. He writes as though he's unaware that we have lost more Agents to the Marenites than we have lost knights to the Scanrans!

Eleni and I send our warmest love to you, to my (again!) pregnant daughter (how in the Mother's Holy Name did you get Alanna with child at <u>her</u> age?), and to our grandchildren,

Myles

Introduction

Gods all bless, Nursemaids of the Tortallan Shadow Service. By offering to train new recruits, you fill a vital role in preserving the security of the realm against all enemies.

Your task is difficult. You will teach your Nurselings that our work is often boring, occasionally dangerous, and always exhausting to the mind and spirit. As you may recall from your training, it cannot be stressed enough that they will not even be able to let friends and loved ones know what they do, let alone the world at large. It is doubtful that they will ever receive public recognition for their efforts. Nevertheless, what we do is vital to the defense of the realm.

No One Is to See This Overview Other Than You, Upon Pain of Imprisonment or Death.

Know that Their Majesties expect everyone in the Shadow Service to do their duty to the Crown.

Father
Chancellor of Information

Tortallan Royal Shadow Service Guide—
Overview

By "John Juggler"

The Chancellor charged me to write a Guide
to train future Nursemaids. After much pleading
with him and the Deputy Chancellor, I instead
wrote this Overview to give the future Guide a
direction, which I now share with you. Read it
carefully, think about what's included and what's
not, and let me know by the usual channels what
I've missed and why it's important. I will be
working closely with you all to create a complete
and proper Guide—not the half-lettered version I
would surely write on my own!

In this Guide, words are to be emphasized—
like <u>eavesdrop</u> and <u>tracking</u>—the first time they're
used. They will be explained later if necessary,
to be certain your Nurselings learn them. You
know them as part of the cant we already use so
often that we may have forgotten we had to learn
them somewhere. That somewhere was at our
Nursemaid's knee, which is now your knee. So

remember to teach those words, among many other things in this Guide.

Once again, if you think I've missed anything, let me know.

JJ

Organizational Chart for the Royal Spy Service

Chancellor of Information - "Father"
|
Deputy Chancellor of Operations - "The Whisper Man"

| Chief Falcon "John Juggler" (1) | Chief Harvester "Stabler" (2) | Chief of Nursemaids "Scarlet" (3) | Chief of Hostlers "Hurrock" (4) |

Deputies to Chief of Falcons, Chief of Nursemaids, and Chief of Hostlers
|
Harvesters Outside Tortall
(generally Diplomatic Attaché or Ambassador)
|
Nursemaids

Sparrows   Hostlers
|
Hostler Trainees
|
Nurselings

For Personal Reference, DO NOT PUBLISH

1) "John Juggler" is Evin Larse of the Queen's Riders.
2) "Stabler" is Stefan Groomsman, head groom for Her Majesty's household.
3) Rebekah Lofts, aka "Scarlet," is Tansy Lofts's great 7-times granddaughter.
4) Ahmet Kemail, aka "Hurrock," is son of former headman, Sunset Dragon tribe.

Who's Who in the Shadow Service

As Nursemaids, most of you have met "Father" (Chancellor of Information), "Scarlet" (Chief Nursemaid), "Hurrock" (Chief Hostler), "Stabler" (Chief Harvester), and me (Chief Falcon) at one time or another. We're the public faces of the Service—do I need to remind you to tell your Nurselings they're not to approach us except under <u>extreme</u> circumstances, like someone is on their way to kill the Queen or steal the Dominion Jewel? (They can approach me, if they think getting a clout upside the head's worth it.) Father's immediate subordinate is the Deputy Chancellor of Operations, known as "the Whisper Man." Most have not met him in this guise, nor will they ever meet him.

The ranks of everybody else are as follows:

<u>Nurselings</u>—The future <u>Sparrows</u> you're training. You're to teach them everything you were taught and everything you've learned over the years as a Sparrow yourself—which should be what we're putting into this Guide. They'll be Nurselings

until you decide they're ready to be tested, and
they pass those tests to our, and your, satisfaction.

Sparrows—Soon as your Nurselings pass their
testing, they're known as Sparrows. Sparrows
do the day-to-day spywork like street-level
intelligence gathering, writing reports, passing
on coded reports and messages, and dealing with
Magpies (informers).

Unless they travel with a caravan or boat as
part of their lawful cover, Sparrows don't travel
on spywork. If they travel for reasons other than
their lawful cover, be sure they know that they
must check with you first. This is for their own
protection as well as ours.

Stress it's likely most of them will be Sparrows
the whole time they're working for us. That's no
reflection on their talents because we can't do our
job if they don't do theirs.

Hostlers—You might recommend some Nurselings
to be trained as Hostlers, who track people,
cultivate possible Magpies and Defectors, go
covertly when we need to really know what's going

on somewhere, and do <u>interrogations</u>. They also, when necessary, do things like <u>pickpocketing, robbery, sabotage, assault,</u> and <u>killing</u>. We don't have a lot of Hostlers because it takes a special type of person to be one.

Many think of Hostlers as the "real spies," which means they think spywork is naught but skulduggery and mayhem. Hostlers are the most visible but least important part of the Service—in fact, using a Hostler when one isn't needed can do everybody more harm than good. Hostler training is covered in a separate Guide because there's no need to plant the idea of swirling cloaks and flashing daggers into your Nurselings' minds!

<u>Nursemaids</u>—That's you, former Sparrows and Hostlers who were selected to be <u>Nursemaids</u>. This job is a hard one for many because it takes a different way of thinking to be a Nursemaid than a Sparrow or Hostler. Nursemaids have three main jobs: (1) training Nurselings, including going with them on missions until you're satisfied they can work on their own as Sparrows; (2) passing on orders and gathering reports from the Sparrows

and Hostlers assigned to you; and (3) developing intelligence by compiling records and reports from Sparrows and Hostlers and from outside sources like schools, temple libraries, and the Hall of Records.

Nursemaids and Nurselings stay at the Nursery, our training school in Corus, until you think your Nurselings are ready to be trained out in the field. The rest of the time Nursemaids live in cities and towns, always under lawful cover. That's because you know who the Sparrows and Hostlers you're responsible for are, along with whom you pass information to and get orders from—information others will go to a <u>lot</u> of trouble to get.

<u>Harvesters</u>—Sometimes a senior Sparrow, Hostler, or Nursemaid is asked to be a <u>Harvester.</u> Harvesters gather information from Nursemaids, put it together, and make sure it gets back to the right people in Corus. When orders are issued, it's also the Harvester's job to pass that on to the proper Nursemaids. Because of their duties and the dangers of carrying secret information

outside Tortall, Harvesters are often Diplomats.
They may also be parts of ships' crews, caravans,
traveling priests—even Players.

Harvesters do not develop intelligence—they
give it a preliminary appraisal and rating and make
sure that it gets safely back to Corus.

Falcons—I'm a Falcon. In fact, I'm Chief Falcon.
Falcons are in charge of the Shadow Service's
operations and intelligence for a territory, both
inside and outside Tortall. Harvesters report all
information they've gathered to send to us, and
take orders to pass on from us. At will, a Falcon
can arrange a meeting with any Sparrow or Hostler
in his or her territory and give them orders or
information deemed necessary. The Falcon's orders
supersede any others, save those given by a Chief,
the Whisper Man, or Father.

Falcons have lawful covers, often owning
homes or businesses in major cities, so nobody
thinks twice about people dropping in on them at
all hours of the day and night.

There may be as few as one Falcon to a
small country we're friendly with like Tyra, or

more than a dozen in an empire where we've had and could again have trouble, like Carthak or the Copper Isles. Falcons report directly to the Deputy Chancellor. Most of the time those reports are written, or if it's really urgent, some kind of magical device like a <u>scrying mirror</u> is used. However, at least once every few years a Falcon has to report in person. Because of that, Falcons need a reason for why they travel out of town on a regular basis—like buying and selling at fairs, or picking up some extra coin as a caravan guard.

<u>Owls</u>—Sometimes we need help with things like magic, special knowledge, or even research that's not in libraries or temple records. That's when we call the <u>Owls</u>—those persons who aren't agents but are kin to the Service and happy to lend a hand, or a paw, or a claw. Many times Owls are mages like Master Numair Salmalín or Master Lindhall Reed, or the Wildmage Veralidaine Salmalín, since mages often have talents like book learning or experience the rest of us don't. But Owls can also be Traveling Merchants, Players, even immortals or animals—especially Gifted ones!

Lawful Cover Versus
Unlawful Cover in Foreign Countries

If possible, all Falcons, Harvesters, Nursemaids, and Sparrows reside in a foreign country lawfully, living and working under their own names as normal residents or subjects. There's a good reason for this—the fewer lies they have to remember, the easier it is not to trip up! (We call this Living Your Cover.) They're also less likely to be mistreated if they get caught engaging in suspicious behavior as a legal resident or subject. In many cases, they may just get sent on their way with no more than a quick clout to the head, rather than being arrested and interrogated. Falcons and Harvesters always possess lawful covers and only engage in criminal acts if there's no other choice.

By contrast, unlawful cover means they're pretending to be somebody they're not, and is only used by Hostlers—usually for quick missions that are illegal anyway. If they're in a country unlawfully, impress on them that if they're caught they will be treated as a spy. They will be thrown in prison (probably indefinitely) and questioned (probably painfully), even in a friendly country.

Learning and Using Codes and Cyphers

Learning how to use codes and _cyphers_ is something you need to teach your Nurselings. Remind them to always use code names, and show them how to let others know your message or report's not forged. Learning to write messages and reports in code and decode them must be as natural as breathing before their training's over.

When you teach your Nurselings codes, be sure they understand those codes are just between you and them. Not everybody in the Shadow Service is taught every code, and codes change frequently. Every code, no matter how difficult, will be broken eventually. _Never Let Them Assume That Their Coded Messages Are Completely Secure._

Cyphers substitute letters and numbers with other symbols. When people first learn to read and write, they sometimes play with switching letters around so _A_ is _Z,_ _B_ is _Y,_ and so on—or maybe they use numbers instead of letters. Other cyphers substitute something less obvious like drawings or marks, and though they seem harder to crack than a letter and number cypher, they're just as easy to break once you know what you're looking at. For instance, a group of rogues who used stick figures as a cypher were caught when Deputy Provost Sherringford Adler figured it out.

Codes use references to other documents in order to be written and read. The classic type of code uses a codebook that always stays in a safe place and changes several times a year. While you can haul a codebook while traveling, it's inconvenient and easy to steal. That's why Hostlers and traveling Harvesters prefer either cyphers or book code. These are a series of letters and numbers that direct the reader to specific words in a specific book—for instance, "3-121" would refer to word 121 on page 3. Any book that both the sender and reader have identical copies of can be used, like printed books that come from the same printer, and it won't rouse nearly as much suspicion if they're found with one. (When I was a Queen's Rider, I used the Rider's Manual issued to all of us when performing Hostler duties.) If the two copies come from different printers, or are books copied out by hand, though, a book code is useless.

There's a new type of code the mages at the Royal University are working on, that they say changes characters according to some kind of number pattern that can only be decoded if you have a magical key. They claim you won't need the Gift to use it, just a phrase that will code and decode perfectly. I won't speak ill of any mages who can turn me into a frog or a tree—but I'm thinking most of us won't be using any fancy uncrackable magic code any time soon!

Sparrow Tracks—Teach your Nurselings that a way to limit forgery of coded messages is by using Sparrow Tracks. These can be dots over particular characters, scribbles on the margins, even a particular symbol scrawled in certain places. These Sparrow Tracks move in a seemingly random pattern from message to message so somebody who has seen the coded messages but isn't aware of where the Tracks go next won't be able to successfully duplicate them. You and your Nurseling will work on a system of unique

Sparrow Tracks that you will readily recognize during their training.

Training—All Nurselings

Before you let your Nurselings out in the field, even under your supervision, they will be expected to demonstrate their abilities in:

Writing Reports—Nobody likes writing reports, but your Nurselings need to learn that a major part of their duties will involve writing and submitting them. Impress on them that their reports keep the realm from harm and can save their life and the lives of those who work with them.

The types of reports you'll teach them to write or deal with include Background Reports, Profiles, Assessment and Appreciations, Urgent Immediate Reports, or the highly confidential Colored-String Reports. Colors for strings are White for immortals; Gray for Gifted animals like the Long Lake Wolf Pack; Red for countries Tortall is at war with, like Scanra; Yellow for countries unfriendly to Tortall but we're not at war with, like Tusaine; Blue for countries friendly with Tortall but we're not at present allied with, like Tyra or the Copper Isles; Green for countries we have an alliance with, like Carthak; and Uncolored Twine for matters inside Tortall.

Researching Information Using Books and Reports—For many, research is as bad as writing reports, though it's necessary. Teach your Nurselings how to skim-read so they can go through reports or books quickly and remember what they've read, how to read a report to separate what they need from the chaff bureaucrats always throw in, and how to dress and act so they fit in when they go to a school or temple library, or the Hall of Records.

Once you're satisfied they're ready, give them a stack of reports or books, telling them to glean as much of one type of information from them as they can in a day. A Nurseling who proves to have a talent and liking for research can be given extra training and put to work in Corus, or under the command of a Falcon outside it, as a Research Sparrow.

<u>Eavesdropping and Lip-Reading</u> are two of the most basic skills Nurselings need to master. Teach them to be very good at doing both, and remembering exactly what was said to put in a report later. Demonstrate effective ways to <u>eavesdrop</u> (listen to conversations without seeming to), both using <u>spy hole</u> (viewing or listening) <u>spells</u> and how to listen unobserved when one isn't handy, along with how to <u>lip-read</u> (tell what somebody is saying by watching the movement of their lips, rather than by hearing them). Don't forget techniques to improve their memories (like how to build a <u>Memory House</u> inside their minds so they can remember things later), as well as exercises to sharpen the ability to report back what they've overheard or lip-read precisely.

Before you move to the next step, your Nurselings must be able to eavesdrop on a half-hour conversation—then write a report, including as much of the conversation as they can remember word for word. They must also be able to sit out of hearing of somebody speaking quietly, and by watching the movement of their lips alone, repeat back to you what is being said for at least five minutes.

Avoiding Eavesdroppers—While you're teaching them how to eavesdrop, you'll also teach your Nurselings how to avoid being eavesdropped on. You're to teach them what to look for that suggests somebody is trying to listen to their conversations, ways to prevent lip-reading, how to detect the use of a spy hole spell without magic, and how to avoid it hearing or seeing them. Your Nurselings will also learn how to use anti-eavesdropping spells, though they shouldn't expect them to be issued except in special cases.

Information-Gathering in Public—Teach your Nurselings how to ask questions without seeming to, how to lead a conversation where they need it to go, and how to find out from several different people if they tell a similar tale to spot if somebody's lying.

After initial training, make arrangements with the Shadow Service's Examiners to take your Nurselings out in public for a test. Tell your charges to uncover some bits of information the Examiners will already have arranged to have planted by rumormongers. There will also be Sparrows in the crowd under orders to deceive your Nurselings so you and the Examiners can judge their success in ferreting out who's lying and who's not.

<u>Dealing with Magpies</u>—Next to writing reports, dealing with Magpies (informers) is every Sparrow's least favorite task. Magpies are jumpy, unreliable, prone to lie or exaggerate for a bigger payday, and will try to yank on heartstrings when they're not trying to bully! Sad to say, they're also our best source of gathering information where we can't place a Hostler safely—so you'll have to train your Nurselings to work with them. If it helps, tell them to be grateful that they can leave recruiting Magpies to the Hostlers.

Every Magpie has a different reason for singing to us, and every Sparrow has a different way of dealing with them. I won't tell you how to teach, but if you'll take a bit of advice? I'd say to treat their Magpies like a ma or da treats a troubled child—gentle when you can be, firm when you must be, as generous as you can be given you've not got much to give, but always remember that despite all you do they could easily go bad.

To test your Nurselings, the Examiners will set up a meet in a public place with some Senior Sparrows playing Magpies. You will not, of course, tell your Nurselings these Magpies are fakes, or that you know the information they're to divulge—just that they are to find out what these Magpies have to offer, and to pay them some pittance for it. You and the Examiners will watch how your charges treat their fake Magpies, and what information they got out of them in their report to you. Be sure they describe the meet in detail, to see if they're telling how it went straight or if they're spinning tales themselves.

<u>Tracking Inside a City</u>—Following, or <u>tracking,</u> a person inside a city is another skill your Nurselings need to get very good at. During training, teach them how to do both <u>open</u>

tracking (somebody who knows they're being followed) as well as the more difficult closed tracking (somebody who shouldn't know they're being followed).

Be sure your charges know there are times when one is preferable over the other: For instance, while they might think they would always want to closed-track a Subject (the person or people being tracked), sometimes it helps to see how the Subject jumps knowing they're being stalked. Tell them to watch how their Subject behaves—who they run to for help, or how they deal with knowing they're being followed.

To test their tracking skills, have them closed-track a Subject for a whole day or night and at the end write a report of their Subject's movements. If they can effectively closed-track within a city, then they shouldn't have any problems with open tracking, either.

Investigation—Part of information gathering involves investigation—that is, searching places a Subject is or was at, or examining something they left behind and figuring from that where they came from and why they were there. This part of your Nurselings' training won't just be you and them—they'll also be taught by Senior members of the Provost's Guard to look for the same things they do to solve crimes.

Stress to your Nurselings: (1) <u>Never Volunteer Any Details,</u> and (2) <u>Pay Utmost Attention to What the Guardsmen and Guardswomen Are Teaching.</u> We of the Shadow Service aren't likely to be as good at investigating as Senior Provost Guards are, but be sure your charges learn as much as they can because it will make them better at their jobs.

Test your Nurselings by having them investigate a room where a Subject lived or worked. Their job is to determine what the Subject did while there, whether the Subject was a foreign spy or not, and if so, to deduce, as best as they can, what this spy was up to. Was it simple intelligence gathering? Recruiting people to work as his spies? Possible <u>sabotage</u>—that is, wrecking the gear or spells that aid and protect the Kingdom? Maybe even <u>assassination</u>—killing off somebody important to the Kingdom in some way?

<u>Resisting Interrogation</u>—At some point, every member of the Service can expect to be subjected to some form of <u>interrogation,</u> being questioned by an official from the local Guard or a foreign spymaster. This can be one of the most unpleasant parts of the job, especially if the interrogation is done in a country that is hostile to Tortall. That's why you must teach your Nurselings the means of resisting both <u>hard</u> and <u>soft</u> interrogations.

Hard interrogations are difficult if you're not prepared for them, and can include intimidation; not being allowed to answer nature's call or to sleep; pain; and magic spells to cause fear, force the Subject to tell the truth, or detect when the Subject is lying. The only good thing about hard interrogations is that they're usually conducted by people who have more faith in the infallibility of their methods than is warranted, and hear what they want to hear so they only expect confirmation.

Soft interrogations, by contrast, usually involve the interrogator being helpful and friendly, to get you to trust him or her. They'll offer tea, ask about family, make you feel like you've got naught to worry about. . . . That's how they ferret out what you're really doing, in the same friendly and concerned way. By the time they're done, you will have told them everything you know and won't even realize how deep in the muck you are!

I'm sure you remember from your training how it didn't sound like that would work at all without the use of some kind of magic, and how well it worked on you even if your Interrogator doesn't have a trace of the Gift or the Sight. It's hard for people in trouble to resist a kindly face and a friendly voice; it may take longer and is harder for most Interrogators to do, but when they have the time and patience, it's very effective.

A classic interrogation ploy is to combine hard and soft interrogation by having one Interrogator be sympathetic, while the other intimidates the Subject. The Provost Guard calls this "Good Dog/Bad Dog" for some reason—and has since time out of mind.

That is why the most important thing you can teach your Nurselings is how to lie convincingly when they're the Subject, and how to determine when the time is right to "surrender" and tell their interrogator the lie they have ready.

At the start of training, you helped your Nurselings build Memory Houses, which are parts of the mind where people can store items to remind them of what they need to remember. A variation on this which can be very effective during interrogation is a <u>Liar's Palace,</u> a mental construct of fake "memories" of who you're pretending to be. If your charges build their Liar's Palace well enough they can even convince people with the Sight they're telling the truth, because they will believe it then!

It's true that few people can live inside their Liar's Palace that completely, but it's not impossible. We know of a highly resourceful spy who recently succeeded in fooling the late Spymaster of the Copper Isles in this way. Despite being dosed with a truth spell and surrounded by fear spells, she convinced the once-unstoppable Topobaw that she was just a simple-minded and bigoted freewoman, worth cultivating as an Informant on the raka! We believe that her actions played a major role in Topobaw's downfall and execution.

Explain to your Nurselings that even if they don't completely believe their Liar's Palace, they'll learn to believe it well enough to at least fool run-of-the-mill interrogators without the Sight. Fortunately, the Sight isn't nearly as common as people believe it is, and few interrogators possess it, since those who do usually find much more lucrative and satisfying outlets for their gods-given power.

During training, you'll stage periodic "mock interrogations" for your Nurselings, which should happen without warning, and range from very basic questioning to pretty hard interrogation. (No torture, thank the Gods, as you want them to succeed.) Rather than a set test, keep track of how your charges handle these mock interrogations. Part of your job as a Nursemaid is to decide if they're ready to go be interrogated by strangers or not.

Note About Hard Interrogation: We don't train people in how to do hard interrogations that involve pain or fear spells, let alone torture. It's been whispered about by other Spy Services that this is what you get when you give women too much power in a country, mostly by those who've never actually faced His Majesty's Champion Sir Alanna or Her Majesty in a fight! They think this makes Tortall somehow "weaker" than they are. They're welcome to continue believing that, same as they're welcome to keep believing that the best answer is one beaten out of somebody. While it's possible that somebody in the Shadow Service has used those types of hard interrogation, it is against Our Royal Majesties' Law, and anyone found doing it will be hauled up on charges before the Chancellor and Deputy Chancellor.

It's not just because we're too "nice" to get our hands dirty, but because it's too often the best way known under the Gods' Realm to develop bad intelligence that will get people killed. Someone in pain will tell their interrogators what they want to hear, not what they need to hear, so acting on that information is always dangerous. We've also found that Spy Services that rely on these tactics are no better than footpads, so it's easy to bribe or blackmail any number of them. The Copper Isles Spy Service was more feared for its brutality than respected for its skill, and got brought down because of thinking like this.

<u>Note About Engaging in Criminal Acts</u>: Unless your Nurselings are chosen to train as Hostlers, they should be strongly discouraged from engaging in criminal acts in the furtherance of their duties as Sparrows. A large part of Hostler training involves when to engage in criminal acts like pickpocketing, lock picking, burglary, sabotage, assault, and <u>spiriting</u> (kidnapping), and how best to do so if needful.

We know that other Spy Services consider our minimizing the additional damage our Hostlers do as a sign of "weakness." Their equivalents to our Hostlers seem to make a point of pride out of how much havoc they can wreak along the way! That's well and good if mayhem is all you wish. However, keep in mind that the King of Tusaine, after an unlawful operation launched by the spymaster in charge in Corus resulted in the deaths of a dozen civilians and the torching of three blocks in the Mire, had him recalled, drawn, and quartered. Perhaps His Majesty of Tusaine was inspired to this act by the receipt of a boxful of the ears of the agents involved in the operation, courtesy of the Whisper Man.

Most Important Lesson of All

Teach your Nurselings that "adventure" is another person's life in deep dung far away. If a charge still hankers after new faces, places, and risks after a month of the dullest Nurseling work you have, talk to me. I will decide if Hurrock has a new Hostler recruit, or Commander Buri has a new Queen's Rider . . . once he's had a chat with one of our mages. Memory Spells or Forget-Me Tonics to make a body unremember his new friends are wondrous things! There's no need to tell the world the little we've taught him.

Note About the Use of Magic in Spywork

by Master Numair Salmalín,
Royal University in Corus

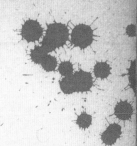

The emphasis in this Guide is on non-magical means of teaching new members of the Royal Tortallan Shadow Service their jobs, even though it does touch on magic in spywork and the use of spelled devices. The reason for that is because I spent years on the run from then Carthaki Emperor Mage Ozorne, and I learned the hard way that using magic when people are looking for you is a bad idea. Active magic is easy for anyone with the Gift or Sight, or using magic-detection devices like we give Hostlers, to see. Passive magic, as used in spy hole spells or forget-me suits, can still be sensed by anyone possessing powerful enough Sight, or with magic-detection devices.

Also, don't think you can just magic your way out of trouble if detected. I am judged to be a powerful mage, but I can be defeated by a hedgewitch if my attention's diverted, I've used up my Gift, or I'm exhausted. Also, all my power doesn't stop an enemy without the Gift from clouting me on the head, drugging my drink, or knifing me if I'm not careful.

If you believe one of your "Nurselings" possesses the Gift or Sight, or even the extremely rare "wild magic" as my wife, the Wildmage, has, inform the Chief of Nursemaids or me personally so we can test them, then train them to be Mage-Spies accordingly.

Numair Salmalín

Spy Reports

November 14, 439

To Myles Olau

By way of Honus Windfeld, innkeeper

The Wandering Bard, Berat in Maren

A gathering of information with regard to
Princess Thayet jian Wilima of Sarain and her
guard, the K'mir Buriram Tourakom, at your
request, information taken from a number of
K'mir, Saren, mixed-bloods, and outlanders

Princess Thayet jian Wilima, former heiress of Sarain

- Adigun jin Wilima, father, King of Sarain, deceased 439
- Kalasin of the K'miri Hau Ma, mother, deceased by suicide, May 3rd, 438
- Thayet, born August 8th, 421 H.E., only issue of marriage of Adigun jin Wilima and Kalasin

Princess Thayet, as heir to the throne, was given a proper Eastern lady's instruction by tutors chosen by her father, including etiquette, dancing, management of a Great House, accounting, history, languages (Common, K'miri dialects, trade talk in the Roof of the World, Carthaki), horseback riding in the Imperial style, hunting with falcons and bows. News from K'mir tradesmen and wandering peddlers reveals that the queen also arranged for the princess, required by the royal wedding treaty to spend three summer months with the queen's people, to learn riding in the K'miri style, combat with sword and dagger, care for horses, forest and plains hunting without royal retainers, tracking, and wilderness cookery.

At 12 the princess was joined by the 8-year-old Buriram Tourakom, called Buri, the child and sister of her mother's sworn K'miri bodyguards. Buriram held their place with the princess as guard, even at court ceremonial occasions. She is permitted to do so under Kalasin's wedding treaty and as part of the blood bond between Kalasin, her child, and

Buriram's family. When Kalasin destroyed herself, Buriram's mother and brother gave their lives so she might proclaim her wrath with the king to the people. Buriram herself has been often wounded in defense of Thayet jian Wilima.

Apparently the addition of Buri was the last feather on the king's burden of grievance with his wife's "barbarian ways." His quarrels with Her Majesty became infamous: she was very popular with the Saren people for her kindness and good works. He brought his mistresses to court and paraded them before the queen and princess at public occasions. He also began a program of persecution of the K'mir, passing laws against them and arresting, imprisoning, and hanging them for newly created crimes.

Kalasin and Thayet did their best to try to influence him, but the nobles and lowland Sarenites found advantages to be had in taking K'mir horses and property.

In December 436, Kalasin sent Thayet to the Mother of Mountains convent, supposedly to tame her wildness, but in reality to keep her from her father's displeasure. In late 437, King Adigun enacted, among other laws, one demanding the K'mir come to the fortresses and register their names no later than April 15th, or be considered in revolt. Kalasin protested, refusing to appear anywhere in the king's company. She ordered his mistresses be thrown out of the palace. Before his ministers could agree according to Saren law, the king ordered her to a convent. Kalasin sent word through the capital of her plans. Two days later, before a crowd of citizens, she ascended the highest tower of the palace, spoke of the king's inhumanity to his people, and leaped to her death. Buriram's mother and brother died defending the doors to her tower room so her protest would go uninterrupted.

By April 439, when Princess Thayet returned to the capital, the king was dead. Our watcher in the convent here in Rachia, where she stayed before her departure, said that no one approached her with regard to remaining in Sarain to fight in the coming civil war. Rather than become a trophy to those in contention for the crown, she chose to accompany Lady Alanna of Trebond, Liam Ironarm, the Shang Dragon, and Coram Smythesson, a man-at-arms, on a quest eastward, out of Sarain. Once they crossed the M'kon River on the eastern border, my sources were able to learn only that they traveled to the Roof of the World and returned from there, to take ship to Tortall. If she was contacted by agents in the mountains, we have no way of discovering it.

There was one small bump, as you will see in the enclosed letters, but it has been taken care of. Her friends in Sarain wish Her Royal Highness all prosperity in her new life.

Buriram Tourakom

- Thiratay Tourakom, mother, tribe K'miri Raadeh, deceased in combat, May 3rd, 438
- Pathom Tourakom, older brother, tribe K'miri Raadeh, deceased in combat, May 3rd, 438
- Susatahan Longprum, father, tribe K'miri Sembou, deceased in combat, 429

Like all K'mir children, she takes her name from her mother's family. Her family is as close to nobility as the K'mir get, apart from the bloodlines of the old royalty, of which Kalasin and Thayet are the last descendants.

Buri's heritage is twice rich in honor for the manner in which her mother and brother died, keeping soldiers from sullying Queen Kalasin's denouncement of the king for his treatment of his people. Such a death is sacred among the K'mir and those who know of K'mir ways. To be stopped from finishing such a death is a great shame to the family of the one who embarked on it.

Thiratay and Pathom now hold places on the roll of honor, to be named on the great holidays. A horsehair is burned for each in the Midwinter fires. As their only descendant, Buri will be able to command the help of any K'mir or ally of the K'miri tribes, and great things will be expected of her. No doubt she will attract the more adventurous members of her people west to Tortall, to serve her and Thayet.

For herself, she is a well-trained warrior, even though she is young, and a fine rider and judge of horses. Her teachers say her manners require polish if she is to go among lowlanders. For those who appreciate a fine maker of compound bows, which require much patience, and a gentle hand with newborn foals and hounds, 'Buri's lack of a feathered tongue is no bad thing.

October 23, 439 H.E.

Skullcap—

It is my understanding that the slut has made her way to Tortall and is throwing herself on the mercies of the milksops there. Mithros only knows what lies she is making up about our situation regarding the rule of the realm, our intelligence gathering there, or anything else she learned before she fled. All we need is for her to convince the boy who is due to take the throne to get charged up with youthful ardor and send a force to do battle for the wronged princess.

Take your team and find some way to deal with the situation. The woman, her so-called K'miri "guard," that Shang fellow, that disgusting female who calls herself a knight, and the servant that rode with them. I don't care how you do it, just leave no tracks. It would be best if they simply disappeared.

Your first half-payment is in the usual place. I believe it is sufficient to satisfy even your greedy heart.

Master Olau, this is the document I
chanced to lay my hands on recently.

Do not concern yourself about the writer
or his correspondents. There are no other
copies, and the writer has been persuaded
that this was a very <u>final</u> course of action
to take.

Harvest Spider

P.S. I tracked down the payment he would
have gotten and gave it in equal shares to
the temples of the Horse Lords, Mithros,
the Great Goddess, the Trickster, and the
God of Shadows, who rules the dead.

H.S.

November 15, 439

Spies of the Merchant Lord in the West,

I write on behalf of the council of K'mir
chiefs, gathered at this time as is our custom
when great decisions must be made. You have
sent your little spies among those who trade
with the tribes and marry among us. They ask
questions with regard to Thayet jian Wilima and
Buriram Tourakom, who have been forced from
this land by the plots and murders of the Saren
lowlanders.

Know this. Thayet is free to go where
she wishes and to live how she wishes. She
understands that she cannot return to the tribes
of the K'mir. As long as she bears her father's
blood the greedy lowland noblemen will use her
to claim the throne. They will search for her
among the forests and grasslands of the K'mir
unless it is known she is not to be found there.
Buriram is still held by her family's oath to
Thayet's mother's line and will remain with her.

Never again will the K'mir bind themselves
to the lowlanders. We gave them a woman of our
most precious bloodline to seal a peace, and their
king gave us theft, oath breaking, evil laws, and
bloodshed. Now we will take back our forests
and grasslands. We will drive the lowlanders
from them. There can be no peace with the noble

born of Sarain. They will learn the price of every drop of blood they have taken from us and our young, down to our newborn foals. Warn the lowlanders if you like. They believe us to be fools. They will learn otherwise.

Our chiefs and their tribes wish all good things to Thayet and Buriram. May they find happiness far from this land of sorrows. We will all meet again, in the lands of the Horse Lords, when the time for mortal fury is done.

Kosal Toalvorn of the K'miri Bantey
Recorder, the Gathered Tribes

Sir, this was in my saddlebag when I went to leave the city upon sending my information to you. I had thought I did a good job in covering my tracks so no one would know of my queries, but it seems I was not so clever as I believed.

H.S.

Name: Musenda Ogunsanwo
Also called: Sarge (arena and Rider nickname)

**Date subject first
reported seen in Tortall:**
January 443

Born 415

Homeland:
Carthak, born of a
West Coast tribe

Family:
- Father Abeid, smith; mother Edo,
  carpenter—parents killed in rebellion
  when Musenda was 8
- 6 children, sisters and brothers taken
  and sold as slaves—1 brother known
  deceased
- Sister-in-law, widowed, 3 children—moved
  to Tortall with her second husband
  Added May 444: settled in Port Legann
- Musenda big for age, sold to gladiator
  training masters and trained for arena
  combats
- No children

Precise description:

Height: 6 feet 5 inches
Build: heavy, muscled
Age: 29 at present date
Hair color: black, cut short to skull
Eye color: brown
Skin color: dark brown

Added markings:

Enough to make even me sick, and I was in
the army:

- Shackle galls, wrists and ankles
- Whip scars, ridges on ridges, all over
his back and sides
- Sword scars: right upper chest, left
of belly button, left upper thigh
- Brand on left shoulder—property of
Carthaki Empire

Occupation:

Gladiator training, lesser arena combats,
430–434
Gladiator combats, 434–443
Caravan guard (caravan Paolin, caravan
Inek), 443–444

Habits of speech:

- while issuing orders, a thundering, splendid
roar; otherwise quiet-spoken; a Common
speaker, not learned

-"lambkins," "my lamb," "ain't," "sweet-lookin'," "darlings"—terms he uses often to those he commands

Physical habits and skills:
-very early riser, goes for loooong runs
-does shadow fighting with weapons, bare fists, kicks
-then bathes in nearest cold river or stream
-good campfire cook
-mends his own clothes and the bits of armor he has
-very good with horses

Combat skills:
-javelin, staff, spear, chain (yes, chain, he wears it around his waist and he brained a pirate with it once), short sword, knife
-bare-knuckles fighting, wrestling, kicks
-can lift a grown man near as big as he is over his head and hold him there

Magic:
none that this Hostler was able to spot
He carries a couple of little doll figures in his kit and burns bits of food in front of them before he settles for

the night—says those are just for his parents. He burns food or incense for them so they know he remembers them.

He spoke openly enough about his family during the handful of times I traveled with caravans where he was a guard. The company promoted him fast, from on trial to second-in-command. They like him. He's steady—gets everyone and everything to where they're going, Master Artan, the owner of Paolin, told me, be they headed to Port Legann or to Persopolis. Artan waved off those Wanted posters on Sarge, saying, "If those Carthaki snakes can't hang on to a man, they shouldn't be allowed to have him."

Three times on my last trip strangers were asking too many questions about Sarge till the big man turned up missing one morning, packs and all. I was sad he ran. It was glorious to see him fight!

—Hostler Low Tide

APPROVED: for service in the Queen's Riders
—Whisper Man
February 444

January 24, 445—ALERT

Fugitive from Carthak,
true name Arram Draper,
Tyran-born

Price on His Head
of 5,000 Thaks in Gold
from Emperor Ozorne

Activity and movement by
Arram Draper to be gathered and
reported at all times, particularly
use of his Gift, which has not
yet been reported.

<u>HOSTLERS:</u> Do not allow yourselves to be observed
by him. He is reported to be a <u>powerful mage.</u> Do not
inspect his belongings or his dwelling, if he has one.

Anyone asking questions with
regard to Numair Salmalín or Arram
Draper is to be reported at once.

Highest-Level Secrecy

All readers must have clearance from Chief Falcon,
Deputy Chancellor of Operations, or Chancellor of
Operations before handling records.

Name: Numair Salmalín

Also called: Arram
Draper (birth name)

Homeland:

Tyra — 7 years

Lived 12 years in Carthak,
  speaks Common with
  slight Carthaki accent

Date subject first reported seen in Tortall:

February 443: Subject was possibly the
  wandering juggler reported in villages
  between Pearlmouth and Fief Oshirom on
  the western bank of the Drell.

March 16, 443: Kourrem Hariq, Bazhir
  wandermage and trusted informant of this
  service, reports encounter with Numair
  Salmalín, vagrant juggler, on western bank
  of the Drell several miles north of Fief
  Oshirom. Unusually for this informant, she

allows him to travel with her as far as north of Fief Skyl's Hook.

Other sightings and reports follow:

Note by Whisper Man: My copies of these appear to have been placed in another of the crates—one more reason to clear out this room

Family:

- Father—Yusaf Draper, cloth merchant, sale, import, export
- Mother—Kabidi Draper, formerly Terrliz
- Brother and wife—Pattel and Zerumy, 3 sons, 2 daughters
- Brother and wife—Haran and Noaia, 5 daughters, 2 sons
- Sister and husband—Kerinna and Dofev, 3 sons
- Sister Adasa, brothers Gellab and Mattan
- Father's father—Metan Draper, cloth merchant, sale, import, export
- Mother's father and mother—Iluya and Hazzel Terrliz, cloth merchant, sale
- Mother's grandmother—Bithua Vivim (grandfather dead), lacework

Added by John Juggler:
- Married May 462: Veralidaine Sarrasri
- Daughter Sarralyn, May 462
- Son Rikash, April 464

<u>Precise description:</u>

Height: 6 feet 4 inches
Build: very thin, had recently lost weight in
    first report
Age: over 20 as of January 24, 445
Hair color: black
Eye color: brown
Skin color: brown

<u>Occupations—past and present:</u>

Teacher, Carthaki University
Student healer, Carthaki University
Street performer
Instructor, Tortallan University
Mage in service to Tortallan Crown
Owl, Shadow Service

<u>Habits of speech:</u>

-talkative concerning academic matters,
    easily distractible concerning such
    things
-polite to elders
-uses educated speech, many references to
    scholars

<u>Physical habits and skills:</u>

-walks great distances
-juggles
-performs sleight of hand

Magic:

~~none~~ posed as having none upon arrival in Tortall

CORRECTION January 24, 445: A powerful mage—treat with all care

Further notes—
anything that may be of use to the shadow service:

June 12, 445, note by the Whisper Man:

Our agents have now gathered a great deal of information about the man calling himself Numair Salmalín, born Arram Draper in Tyra. He is a strong mage from the university at Carthak, perhaps one of the greatest according to what my agent was able to read in their documents. Emperor Ozorne has a price on his head for high treason and now demands Their Majesties return Salmalín to him upon pain of war. Given the project Salmalín is now working on with Their Majesties' approval, the Carthaki emperor will have a long wait.

Name: Veralidaine Sarrasri
Also called: Daine

Date subject first reported seen in Tortall:
March 22, 449: Hostler Onua, the Cría
horse fair in Galla. Hired the girl to
bring ponies to palace for Queen's
Riders, learned her story on the way

Homeland:
Town called Snowsdale, in Galla

Family:
- Sarra Beneksri, mother, slain by bandits, March 449
- Benek Todorsra, grandfather, slain by bandits, March 449
- ~~Father unknown~~

Added by Owl Numair: Sarra ascended to the Divine Realms and was made minor goddess of local mountain women, southwestern Galla and northeastern Tortall

Added by Owl Numair: Weiryn, father, minor hunt-god of southwestern Galla and northeastern Tortall

-Married May 462: Numair Salmalín
-Daughter Sarralyn, May 462
-Son Rikash, April 464

<u>Precise description:</u>
Height: 5 feet 5 inches
Build: thin
Age: 13 at first report
Hair color: brown, curly
Eye color: blue-gray
Skin color: fair

<u>Occupation:</u>
Assistant to Queen's Riders
    horsemistress, Onua Chamtong,
    March 449–spring 450
Assistant to Numair Salmalín on
    behalf of the Riders and the Crown,
    July 450–July 451
Assistant to Numair Salmalín and
    special envoy to Carthak on behalf of
    the Crown, September 451
Special mage in the employ of the Crown,
    October 451 to present

<u>Habits of speech:</u>
-soft-spoken, polite
-says "odd's bobs," "oh glory," "mouse
    manure," "my heart bleeds buttermilk"

Physical habits and skills:
- horse care, tracking, hunting, fishing, camp cookery, sewing

Combat skills:
- longbow and crossbow archer (<u>good</u> archer)
- sling (<u>good</u> sling)

Magic:
We met Numair on the road. He believes she has that wild magic he is forever going on about, and I for once agree.
                        —Onua, spring 449

Daine is certainly a wildmage, bound to mortal animals, able to communicate with immortal creatures, invaluable to the realm. She is also a demigoddess.
                        —Whisper Man, November 452

Remaining records doubtless somewhere else in this room! Note to myself—do <u>not</u> leave papers where children can get at them!—W.M.

Name: Kuni Yoro

**Date subject first
reported seen in
Tortall:**
  September 456

Homeland:
  Saikai, Eniwa
  Island, the
  Yamani Islands

Family:
  - Hostler Bifu says
  his people can't learn anything of Yoro's
  family. When his Sparrows ask anything
  careful-like in or near Saikai village, they
  get nothing at best, and threats at worst.
  Bifu told them to drop it before they
  risked themselves. In any case, she left
  home at 5 and was sent to the Imperial
  Palace.
  - No children that we know of.

Precise description:
    Height: 5 feet even
    Build: lean
    Age: 18, maybe 20
    Hair color: black
    Eye color: brown
    Skin color: gold

Occupation:
    Sewing and embroidery trainee, Saikai village
    Seamstress, Imperial Palace embroidery
    trainee
    Seamstress and embroideress, Princess
    Shinkokami and princess's ladies student,
    Eastern-style embroideries, royal embroiderers

    She is Princess Shinkokami's seamstress
    and chief embroiderer, sewing and caring
    for the Yamani gowns Her Royal Highness
    brung with her. She sews and embroiders
    most beautifully. If there are messages in her
    stitches, no one can make them out. They
    seem to be only embroidery, so she doesn't
    pass word to her contacts that way.

Habits of speech:
    Very polite as the Yamanis are, looks at the
    ground when she speaks to the nobility, looks
    aside when talking to the rest of us. Her

Common is very good. When she talks here in the palace she has an accent and fumbles for words, but Sparrows in the city report she speaks well enough when she is shopping or talking with men in the streets. Not that she goes with men. Sparrows say she is interested more in women than men, but she goes with no one.—Stabler

Physical habits and skills:
Like all the Yamanis, she bows often, deep for the nobles, not as deep for the wealthy, just a little deep for the rest of us. She walks in tiny steps.

Combat skill:
She can play the fan-throwing game, even the one using the fan with blades for ribs. Sparrow Ghost reports that sometimes the princess will ask her to dance with the blade fan, and Yoro whirls it all around her body, open and closed.

Magic:
None seen so far. Numair detects none.

Everyone who sends me reports believes
Yoro is a spy for the Yamani emperor.
Hostler Bifu says in his report that the
imperial spy service trains its people in the
palace, where they practice detecting spies
placed on the emperor. Yoro has the perfect
cover. She doesn't have much heavy work
for the princess, so she can study Eastern
threadwork with the ladies, and wander
and ask questions. No one is curious
because she is foreign. She is even allowed
to go to the market to buy cloth, thread,
and notions. Hostler Spear with the royal
Progress says Yoro often talks with soldiers
and servants. Those she talks with say she
asks about who's who, and what nobles own
the fiefs they pass, and what the court is
like, and how things are done.

Let's keep her. Keep her, find how she
stays in touch with her Yamani masters,
and read their letters. This is our first
chance to get near a Yamani spy, and one
trained up to it from a child at that. Grab
the chance. Do everything we can to feed
her false sweets to send home and keep her
with us. She might lead us to other Yamani
spies, too. And we can read the emperor's
letters.

　　—Stabler

From the Whisper Man

To Stabler and John Juggler

August 23, 457

Regarding Kuni Yoro

I agree. Let's keep this one and see who she
leads us to. Do what you and John Juggler see fit
to put a watch on her, keeping in mind the problems
we've had with imperial spies in the past. Check with
Owl—mayhap we can place some watch spells on her.
We shouldn't use lesser mages for this.

From Owl
To the Whisper Man, the Singing Man,
and John Juggler

September 30, 457

Regarding Kuni Yoro

Forgive me, my friends, but magic
is not an option. She wears some manner
of token on her person, and the same
is placed among her belongings, which
deadens any spells completely. From its
structure it seems to be multiple layers of
spells, locked together in such a fashion
that it would take weeks for me to pick
them apart, if I even could. If I tried, I
am certain that she would be alerted to
my meddling. She would certainly know
if I tried to smash it. I know of no other
mage in Tortall who could do even that.

My deepest regrets, of course. If there
ever comes a time when subtlety is no
longer preferred, I would like to examine
those spells at leisure.

From the Whisper Man
To Stabler and John Juggler

With regard to the response by Owl

October 15, 457

Regarding Kuni Yoro

Well, that's that, then. We'll go at her the old-fashioned way. Let's see about getting some female Sparrows around her own age among the servants in the Progress and working around the princess's suite when they return.

<u>Name:</u> Padraig of haMinch
<u>Also called:</u> Stone Fist by
  men who served under
  him in the army

<u>Date subject first reported</u>
<u>seen in Tortall:</u> native born

<u>Homeland:</u>
  Tortall, duchy of Great
  Minch

<u>Family:</u>
  - The haMinch clans of the northeastern
    mountains
  - Hanaa al Naz of the Bazhir tribe Oldest
    Tale, wife—dead with two children, pox
    epidemic 451
  - Duke Gelban, oldest brother, married Jennett
    of Aili
  - Suvanna, sister, married Duke Cammare of
    Marqueran, Galla
  - Gillin, brother, married Honorine of
    Marqueran, Galla
  - Padrach, nephew
  - Deava, brother, married Amorelle of Anak's
    Eyrie

- Mairgred, sister, married Lord Slaiden of Nicoline
- Deonaid, sister, vowed to the Goddess as Mother, the City of the Gods

There is more family, but you may check the haMinch books for it—his brothers and sisters have given him plenty of nieces and nephews.

Precise description:

Height: 6 feet 2 inches
Build: hard, muscled
Age: 55 in 459 H.E.
Hair color: gray and black, worn in a horsetail
Eye color: brown
Skin color: tan, weathered—an outdoor man

Occupation:

Page, 414
Squire, 418
Knight, 425
Captain in command of foot company, 425
Captain in command of armored company, 428
Colonel in command of division, 432
General in command of southern army, 437
Retired from service, 441

Habits of speech:
- northern mountain burr
- occasional Bazhir expletives

Physical habits and skills:
- great walker, hiker, mountain climber, fisherman
- cannot hunt well, traps
- knows how to survive in the mountains and in the southern desert
- knows plants for medicine and food in both
- knows desert's dangerous spiders, lizards, serpents, sand traps
- has fought spidrens, hurroks, two giants (before escaping, he says), and killer unicorns—witnesses confirm one giant, hurrok flock, and two unicorns. He and the pages were escorting Her Majesty and her ladies when the killer unicorns attacked.

Combat skills:
- broadsword, longsword, two-handed sword, war hammer, double-bladed axe
- maces of all sorts
- scimitar
- longbow, crossbow
- boxing, wrestling

Magic: none

Belongs to the powerful and conservative haMinch clan but has very little interest in politics. Prefers to spend idle time with Shang warriors, Princess Shinko and her ladies, or any Bazhir in Corus.

Served in the army with honor, mostly in the desert—he is well thought of in military circles, even if they feel he went a little "sand-happy."

Has many friends among the Bazhir and took a Bazhir wife—when she died with their daughters in an Itching Pox epidemic, Padraig lost heart for desert life and retreated to his house on family lands in the north, leaving when summoned to be training master.

Those who have approached him for intrigue on either the conservative or Their Majesties' side have both come away empty-handed.

There will be a packet of letters passed to you at the Guild party tonight. Your signal to your contact is to dance only the Lover's Knot, turning aside any other invitation. In return, your contact will offer to assist you with your cloak. This contact is not trained and may drop the papers or show them openly, but necessity dictates her use, and I trust you can cover any mistakes. I need the originals, and a set of copies passed to agent Bluebird, as soon as may be.

Message received, will obey, but the Lover's Knot? Do they even play that fussy old thing anymore? I'm afraid I don't recall it.

They will play it tonight, and many dances begin in the same or in a similar way, so keep a weather eye. Couples take hands to form a large circle of four-person rings, see the diagram. All step in, toward the middle of their ring of four, and raise their hands up by their shoulders. All step out and drop their hands by their sides. This figure is repeated. Then all release their hands, turn to their own partner, and take right hands. The gentleman turns the lady under his arm as gentleman and lady switch positions. All four take hands and step in and out again. Now each gentleman takes right hands with the lady of the other couple and turns her under his arm as they switch positions. At this point, each couple is now standing where the other couple began. Each couple then adopts the dance hold, which, far from being fussy, troubled a number of marriages when it first became popular: Partners face each other. The gentleman's right hand is at the lady's waist, and her left hand rests on his shoulder. His left hand supports her right, out to the side, and they move their feet in a one-two-three, front-side-together pattern while turning, while at the same time progressing sunwise around the larger circle. (If that is not dizzying enough, in a smaller hall they form two circles, one inside the other.) After eight counts, the couples take hands with their new neighbors to form a four-person ring again. And it progresses in this fashion.

From Hostler Veery to the Whisper Man

Trainee Capriole did very well last night, finding reasons not to dance without slighting anyone who asked, quickly hiding the dropped papers with her skirt, and including, unasked for, a shrewd report on her contact when she turned the letters over to me. In my opinion, she can be sent safely to the Yamani court and used in low-level work such as this.

December 3, 441
From Sparrow Hearth
To Nursemaid Beehive

By your order, I enclose selections of
Master Hobart Cusyner's personal diary,
which I have tested for the standard
invisible inks. There are none. Likewise,
no hiding spells gave themselves away to
my inspection using the magicked stone
you lent to me. I enclose it in this packet,
with thanks. I also reviewed the diary for
hidden codes as I copied these pages for
you but found none. Perhaps a more crafty
code breaker would see one where I failed.

   Truly, I believe that whoever
suggested to the Shadow Service that
Master Hobart might be a spy must have
spent a night or two in the Master's wine
cellar. Yes, he deals with many foreign
merchants, but this is because he is forever
coming up with new dishes with which to
do Their Majesties honor and make their
court famous. During those times when
I have accompanied him to market and to
warehouses, I have never seen him pass

over any sort of message. While he can cut up a beef so precisely that no shred of meat is left on the bone, in dealings outside the kitchen his hands shake badly. He could not pass a note to a stranger and I not see it.

Master Hobart is an annoying, carping, exacting old fussbudget, but he is a brilliant cook, perhaps the best in the Eastern Lands. He is <u>utterly</u> devoted to the Crown. He has also been more than kind to my family and to the families of those who work under his supervision. I felt vile in reading his precious diary and copying his secrets. Please say I shan't have to do it again.

Copies of assorted pages from different parts
of <u>the diary of Master Hobart Cusyner,</u>
Master Cook at the Royal Palace in Corus
Taken by Sparrow Hearth at the request
of his Harvester, Beehive

◆ ◆ ◆ ◆

June 1, 441 H.E.

They want a great feast! I cannot believe
it! The realm still suffers from the famine
caused by overuse of the Dominion Jewel. I
know the Jewel saved us during the events
on Coronation Day. It kept the realm from
tearing itself to pieces in last year's great
earthquake, yet there was a famine last
summer as the price. And now, with people
near starving as they wait for this summer's
crops to ripen, I must prepare a feast to
impress ambassadors and guests from other
realms. It is a way to help them believe that
Tortall remains proof against her enemies
despite our troubles.

A royal command is a royal command,
and this is the first such request Their
Majesties have made of me. Mithros who
commands the fire and the Goddess who
governs the kitchens witness it, my staff and
I will not fail Their Gracious Majesties!

♦　♦　♦　♦

June 2, 441

Of all my undercooks, Mistress Judita
has offered a good idea for a subtlety. It is
a cockatrice—
a monster that
combines a rooster
with a pig.

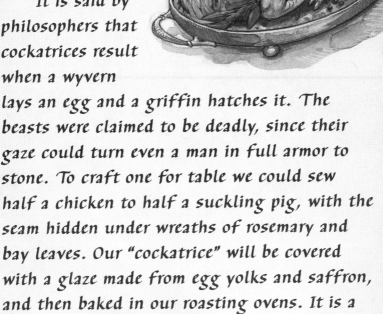

It is said by
philosophers that
cockatrices result
when a wyvern
lays an egg and a griffin hatches it. The
beasts were claimed to be deadly, since their
gaze could turn even a man in full armor to
stone. To craft one for table we could sew
half a chicken to half a suckling pig, with the
seam hidden under wreaths of rosemary and
bay leaves. Our "cockatrice" will be covered
with a glaze made from egg yolks and saffron,
and then baked in our roasting ovens. It is a
most excellent thing the real cockatrices were
exiled to the Divine Realms, so we need not
worry that they will attend the banquet and
criticize our creations!

If they are successful, once we have
introduced our cockatrices at the high table, I

shall employ them again at the tables for lesser nobles and those of the merchant class. They will be amusing at Midwinter, I know.

◆ ◆ ◆ ◆

June 3, 441

Trouble again! A scullery maid was carrying one of my baking pans to the sink for washing. Unfortunately, some beef-witted lout had spilled grease on the floor! Time after time I tell my staff that spills lead to accidents. Do they heed me? That poor girl slipped on the grease and went head over heels. One of my best ceramic pans was shattered. Shards flew everywhere. We tossed a pot of soup for fear that sharp pieces had fallen into it. Worst of all, the girl broke her leg. She will be of little use for several weeks. I must hire and train a new wench to keep her place for her, and buy a new pan.

◆ ◆ ◆ ◆

June 4, 441

I have designed an illusion dish. I will take the uncooked eggs of many birds—not just chicken eggs, but those of quails, geese, swans, and so forth, so my eggs will be of various sizes

and colors. I will then make holes in the shells
with a pin and blow out the contents, saving
them for other dishes. Into the hollow shells I
will have Mathy the undercook place a mixture
of sweetened almond milk and gelatin. We shall
leave the filled eggs in our cold room to set
for a day. Peeled, we will have white, yolkless
"eggs" that seem perfectly normal until they are
tasted. Then let visitors marvel at how sweet
and mild our birds are!

◆　◆　◆　◆

June 5, 441
　　Urchins are a good side dish, but we
cannot have sea urchins. The capital is too far
from the sea to risk their transport. We shall
serve "land urchins." Instead of hedgehogs,
which are scarce, ours shall be made of pork.
The undercooks will chop it very fine, then
mix it both with sweet spices—cinnamon,
nutmeg, clove, and mace—and raw eggs. Next
they will sculpt the mixture into small land
urchins about the size of a child's fist.
　　For spines, we slice almonds lengthwise
into slivers and set them in the "urchins'" back
and sides. Eyes are made with cloves. Then we
bake the whole in a hot oven while our clock
ticks off three-quarters of the hour. I would

defend that device with my own life, at need. I thank King Jasson of glorious memory for loving his supper so much that he graced the palace kitchens with it when he captured one.

◆ ◆ ◆ ◆

June 6, 441

How can I produce a feast on a pittance? On one hand, they want me to serve a meal that will be the talk of the Eastern Lands. On the other, they require I do not overspend. They cannot have it both ways! Does our seneschal think rare spices grow on trees? Well, actually they do, but not here, which is why they cost so much. He even said, "Fear not, Master Cook, you will think of something. You always do." He is right, I always think of something, but this time I am not certain Their Majesties will approve. They are young. What if they are like His Majesty's late father and mother, and not overfond of surprises?

◆ ◆ ◆ ◆

June 7, 441

Now the butchers say they cannot get me a good suckling pig until the month's end. It will be too late then! What can I use in its stead?

◆ ◆ ◆ ◆

June 8, 441

The new spit boy fell asleep while he turned the beef roast for tonight's dinner. Luckily, Judita saw and woke him before half the meat was burnt and the other half raw. She gave him a scolding he will not soon forget. She does very well in her work as an undercook. I must keep my eye on her. Normally Undercook Ingeram is in charge of meat and would watch the spit boy, but I sent him to talk to the royal huntsmen about game needed for next week. The spit boy took advantage of his absence. I instructed Judita to put him to scrubbing pans in addition to his other duties.

◆ ◆ ◆ ◆

June 9, 441

As well as suckling pigs, I cannot get enough of any one small bird—quails, pigeons, doves, larks, ortolans, partridges—to make pies for everyone. I will use a mix, and call the resulting pies "a medley of small birds." Our guests will believe I have done this on purpose and not because I could not obtain enough birds. To the mix I will add a bit of the new southern spice, cumin, that I bought in secret last month. Most of our diners will not have had it in their food before. If I am careful with the amount, it will be pleasantly new, not unpleasantly so.

One of the secrets of being a master cook is to make those you serve believe that all you do is done deliberately, with great struggle and midnight journeys in search of the correct ingredients. If they don't know how you achieve your meals, they will come to see you as being someone close to a mage. If your food is to their taste as well, you will never want for a place to work. So my father taught me and so I teach my own cooks. They may work out their own mysteries. No law is written that I must hand over all of my secrets.

◆ ◆ ◆ ◆

June 11, 441

I finally have the entire menu for the feast decided. Thank the gods, I will be able to get a suckling pig after all.

◆ ◆ ◆ ◆

June 12, 441

Problem after problem! I was just told

that Carthak's ambassador hates spit-roasted boar. Why can foreigners not eat like civilized folk? It was to be the centerpiece of the second course! I was to make sugar-coated and gilded gauze wings for it, and sew three gilded roosters' tails to its bum in place of its normal tail. Now, what may I serve instead?

◆ ◆ ◆ ◆

June 13, 441

All that may be prepared ahead of time is done. Recipes are written for those who read, and those who do not read must ask the readers for help! A master timetable is drawn up, with lesser timetables for each area of the kitchens. Everyone knows what to do and they <u>will</u> do it, or they will answer to me.

◆ ◆ ◆ ◆

June 14, 441

One of my best undercooks is ill! Not Judita, thank all the gods. I could not manage without her level head. No, it is Mathy. He is the best at making pies, and we have so many pies! I must oversee those myself, as if I will not be half-mad with all else!

My prayers to our hunt god Herdun were

answered. The hunters brought us a buck
deer. It is lean, but a night's steeping in wine
and spices will make the flesh tender. With
the gods' will, the Carthaki ambassador will be
pleased. But how could Mathy do this to me?

◆　◆　◆　◆

June 16, 441

Gods all bless us, the feast is over. Those
foreign diplomats returned to their embassies
belching and talking of how well fed we
are. "So much for the tales of famine!" the
Carthaki ambassador is said to have told his
captain-at-arms. We cooks left an offering in
our little shrines for Mithros and the Great
Mother. They treated us well today.

Nor were the gods the only ones to
be generous. As we finished our supper,
Seneschal Wellam entered the kitchen. He was
actually smiling. He placed a fat purse on
the table before me. "Their Majesties' thanks
to you and your staff, Master Hobart," he
said. "I am instructed to say that you have all
done the realm good service, and to ask that
this purse should be divided between you, as
you see fit." He looked at my people. "Very
fine work!" he told them, and then he left us.
I did not torment them by holding the purse

back until I could write up the contents and list who received how much. I called upon Mistress Judita to help me to distribute the coin and made certain everyone received a fair share, from her to the spit boys. They had all earned every copper of it.

❖ ❖ ❖ ❖

August 23, 441

That craven, fawning hedge pig! I will go to Bartly about this! It cannot be legal! Something <u>must</u> be done! One of the undercooks, Ranulf, just left me. (Little loss, the man produced a pie crust as heavy as lead and couldn't season a sauce to save his life!) But he secretly copied my recipes, and he is using them, <u>my recipes,</u> recipes <u>stolen</u> from me. He means to hire on as head cook to some wealthy Corus upstart whose wife wants to boast that her cook serves food the equal of that served at court!

Ranulf has stolen my name and my reputation! No one will believe that I did not sell recipes meant only for Their Majesties' table, or that I did not serve them recipes from those of lesser persons! I will be cast out with no good word from any court official. No one will hire me without the recommendation of my previous employers! I will be made to cook for eating houses, my reputation dragged through the mud. Judita says I must take my case to the magistrates, but I have no coin with which to hire a man of law, who understands these things. My savings went to send my nieces and nephews to school.

My days in these beloved kitchens are numbered. How long before that scut destroys me?

Added long after the clock chimed midnight:

I was awake when Mathy knocked upon my door. With him were a fellow masked in black and that maggot-pie Ranulf! I snatched up a carving knife I had been sharpening to ease my mind, but Mathy bade me to calm myself and asked if they might enter. Once inside, the masked man locked my door. Mathy ordered Ranulf to give my recipes to me.

Ranulf hesitated to obey. The man in the mask prodded him in the back. Ranulf took a dirty wad of papers from inside his tunic and thrust them at me. He jumped at a second prod from the man in the mask and said, "There's no other copies. This is the only one."

I took the papers and leafed through them. They were all my recipes, all in

Ranulf's vile writing. I threw them on the fire. "How do I know you won't use them again from memory?" I asked.

"This hedge pig is going on a journey," Mathy said, and cuffed Ranulf's ear. "We go to put him on a ship, be assured, Master Hobart. He'll be a long time coming back."

"If he dares, but you don't, do you, laddy?" asked the man in the mask. Though it was Mathy who had cuffed him, Ranulf flinched away from the masked fellow.

"None of us in the kitchen want to work for anyone but you," Mathy explained to me. "So I looked up my friend here, and I explained our problem. He knows a bit of this and a bit of that. He helped me find and remove Hedge Pig from his hideout and make his travel arrangements."

"And who might you be?" I asked the masked fellow, suspicious that a man who spoke with the accent of the Lower City ran loose in the palace so late at night. His eyes were familiar to me—hazel with long lashes. They reminded me of those of the Lioness's husband, Baron Cooper. Could it be?

"Someone as is very partial to your soups, Master Hobart," the man replied. "And beggin' your pardon, but it's time for us to be off." He and Mathy gripped Ranulf, each by one arm, and took him away. I locked up for the night. The next morning I rose, feeling thoughtful about my undercook and a crafty fellow who walked the palace halls in a mask, yet talked of tasting my soups. Before I did anything that day, I went to the Trickster's shrine and made an offering, since such a quick change in my fortunes could only be his work.

I will not ask Mathy about his friend. I would hate for him to feel he must lie to me. I am very nearly positive he would lie if I did ask.

◆ ◆ ◆ ◆

August 24, 441
Judita's candied violet petals will be perfect for the subtlety of a castle in the third course. They will add texture and color to its walls, as well as a delicate flavor. She has many clever ideas. Nuts will serve as boulders and spun sugar ribbons as flags. The design is my own, but I will leave the decoration of it to her.

◆ ◆ ◆ ◆

August 25, 441

    I must arrange for delivery of more flour from the royal granary.

◆ ◆ ◆ ◆

August 26, 441

    After the feast, I must get more large cooking pots. Bartly will complain about the expense, no doubt!

◆ ◆ ◆ ◆

August 27, 441

    I have decided to include gooseberry tarts. Her Majesty loves my gooseberry tarts and such beauty should be made happy. Her Majesty is so gracious that it is a pleasure to do any little thing to make her smile. I also did not know her preferences so well when she bore our heir, Prince Roald. I will make it up to her now that she carries a second child.

◆ ◆ ◆ ◆

August 29, 441

    How can I produce a great feast without help? Mathy's assistant now informs us he cannot be here for the next few weeks! His wife was just delivered of a child, and without female relatives to look after things—he is from Whitethorn—he must stay home to care for her, the new baby, and his other children. Why could she not wait a week to give birth, instead of upsetting all my plans? Has she no sense of timing?

Well, there is nothing for it. I shall pay for a servant for their house out of my own pocket. Mathy cannot spare the fellow, and I do owe Mathy a favor, after all. The pastries are too important for Mathy to be short-handed.

◆　◆　◆　◆

August 30, 441

Gods bless us, the feast is today!

◆　◆　◆　◆

September 1, 441

I think I will sleep for a week. The court loved the food. We received great praise, but I will admit here that it gets worrisome, trying to outdo myself time after time. Still, it is not for nothing that I am called the greatest cook in Tortall. Once again Their Gracious Majesties sent a fat purse to us, and the staff raised their cups in salute to me. It is all most gratifying.

I have placed copies of my feast menus in the back of this book, so I will be able to see what I served Their Majesties on the most important occasions. There must be no repetitions in the upcoming banquets this year or next, not at the high tables.

◆ ◆ ◆ ◆

September 2, 441

With the harvest coming in, we must make cider from the apples and perry from the pears. It is also time to put up fruits and vegetables to keep against the long winter, and make dandelion wine. There's winter verjuice to prepare, the potted meats, fruits preserved in honey, soft cheese in oil, pickled meat and fish, and pickled eggs and cucumbers. Our next large feast will not be until Her Majesty gives birth, though of course there will be important guests at court dinners before then. Those are simple affairs and grant us plenty of time to prepare for the winter. I cannot imagine how lesser folk manage without the great cold cellars beneath this palace. I am exceedingly grateful for them, particularly after the famine. No one here goes hungry if I have anything to say about it!

◆ ◆ ◆ ◆

November 8, 441

Goddess be praised, Her Majesty is safely delivered of a beautiful little girl! With mother and infant thriving, it is time for a grand banquet to honor them both. With the famine we could not celebrate Prince Roald's birth as we wished, so our welcome for Princess Kalasin will be an occasion for great feasts and celebrations throughout the realm! Not just the finest food and drink, but fireworks, great displays of magic, plays, and assorted entertainments are planned here in the city. Actors, singers, musicians, and many other entertainers will be hired. While my sole responsibility is the court's banquet, I also have been asked for suggestions by those who must prepare feasts for three different guilds. I cannot help but be proud that my reputation has spread so far. I must also take care that I am not so occupied with assisting others that I fail to give Her Young Highness my very best efforts!

◆ ◆ ◆ ◆

November 9, 441

So many people will be here for the

celebration that my feast will really be two feasts—an elaborate one for the court, visiting royalty, nobles, and ambassadors, and a second for more common folk. Both will overflow with good things to eat, so that those who are present will talk of their meal to their children and grandchildren.

❖　❖　❖　❖

November 10, 441

I have created a delicious new soup for the lesser feast and based on a hunch, I have named it George Soup. I confirmed that Baron George Cooper, husband to the King's Champion, was truly once a common man of the Lower City. There are rumors that he is also the true spymaster to Baron Sir Myles of Olau's official one, and that he makes friends everywhere he goes, on the chance that they might be of use to him. I also know Mathy chooses his friends very carefully. I think that Mathy's commoner friend in the black cloth mask, the one who saved my recipes and my reputation and said he liked my soups,

was Baron Cooper himself in disguise! If I am wrong, he will only think I am trying to curry favor with a noble, and there will be no harm done. If I am right, he will know I have thanked him.

My George Soup is made from poultry cut into quarters, bacon fat, onions, breadcrumbs, wine, chicken livers, verjuice, vinegar, and assorted spices and herbs. It is very flavorful but sits easily on the belly.

◆　◆　◆　◆

November 11, 441

I sent Assistant Cook Ingeram to the royal hunters with my order for all the venison I need for the feast. He will also give them my needs for game birds and small game animals. They will be busy lads in the coming week!

◆　◆　◆　◆

November 12, 441

In honor of the queen and Princess Kalasin, we shall do a subtlety of a mother bird in a golden nest with two young—a larger, feathered chick for Prince Roald, and a smaller, downy bird for the princess. A branch of gingerbread with candied sugar glaze shall bear the father bird, His Majesty. This is another good idea from Judita. I find myself depending on her for more and more. She is a most reliable person for one of her years.

◆　◆　◆　◆

November 13, 441

The kitchen help is grumbling, but I am insisting that every pot, pan, and kettle be thoroughly scrubbed before the feast. I shall check each of them myself before we begin to cook. I want no unpleasant surprises, such as crusts from old meals, and we will need to use much of what we have. I am still tempering the new pots I purchased.

◆　◆　◆　◆

November 14, 441

    The town merchants cannot be counted on. I need fresh eels, yet the fishmonger I always use is not sure he can get enough for me in time, and this after all his promises! Well, perhaps it is time I spread my business about a bit. If he cannot do the task, I shall find someone who will.

◆ ◆ ◆ ◆

November 16, 441

    We have done it before, but it is so popular that we will do it again. I will serve a peacock in its plumage. The look on the faces of the feasters when the peacock is brought in is a sight to behold. We can gild the tail silver and gold, alternating, in salute to Mithros and the Great Goddess.

◆ ◆ ◆ ◆

November 17, 441

    Mathy will not be here to assist with the feast! Before our feast was scheduled, I gave him leave to go to Godsfork to assist at the wedding supper of some cousin of his. Now that I need him, I am honor-bound to let him go. This is what comes of being a gracious employer. I had no idea that Her Majesty would be delivered of her daughter at the same time! I wonder how many more unwed relatives Mathy has?

◆　◆　◆　◆

November 18, 441

The sauces are all finished and safe in the cold cellar. That will save time in preparation the day of the feast. All we will need to do then is heat them, pour them out in the cradle-shaped dishes we used for Prince Roald's birthing supper, and serve.

Later that day

My head! My poor, aching head! My sauce cook just told me that he has been offered the post of head cook to the lord of his home in Arenaver. He will leave immediately, now that the sauces are done! What am I to do? None of his assistants are ready to succeed him, and I cannot face Midwinter without a head sauce cook! He says he is too old for the pace of things in the palace, and he misses his relatives in Arenaver. _He_ is too old! What of _me_? I am ten years older than he if I am a day, but you don't see <u>me</u> complaining of age and retirement!

I had best take myself to the healer for a headache tea. I have no time for illness.

Where will I find a head sauce cook for Midwinter Festival?

◆ ◆ ◆ ◆

November 20, 441

Feast today.

◆ ◆ ◆ ◆

November 22, 441

Another grand banquet, another awed court. Judita, Ingeram, and the rest of the staff outdid themselves. Their Majesties were very generous with their reward. And now I am taking three days to myself, largely to sleep.

<u>That night:</u>

My stars! I returned to my rooms this same night to find a long, wide wooden box. It contained rows of plump bottles, each bearing the name of the costliest, most flavorful, most difficult to find spices of the Copper Isles, the Yamani Islands, and Carthak! It is a treasure beyond belief! With it was a note that read only, "Your George Soup is very fine." Gods bless the man! I vow I shall serve it whenever he is at court!

◆　◆　◆　◆

November 28, 441

I just examined the records from the feast. I can't believe how much wine was consumed. Remarkably, the red was more popular than the white. I must order a great deal more from the southern fiefdoms, to ensure there is plenty for the winter months. Of course Bartly will grumble at the cost. Perhaps he is incapable of smiling. Was he born that way, or might it come with the job of being seneschal?

Killing Device
Reports

Reports sent on to the Chancellor and
the Whisper Man by Fast Courier

April 10, 459 H.E.

Chancellor and Whisper Man,

Both documents are triple-coded. I request
Hostlers on detached duty, the best you have,
fluent in Scanran, woodcraft, and codes,
and some good mages able to deal with both
educated mages and local hedgemages. Word is
getting around about these things—I've even
heard whispers among local soldiers. Dunbar
and Kaaber are a good hundred miles apart
at the least, with Anak's Eyrie another fifty
miles to the east of Kaaber. That's too far for
the latest scare tale to spread in less than a
week. I think the mages of Scanra have found
themselves some manner of new monster to help
them fight us.

I need the supplies and help as soon as may
be. Please alert Their Majesties.

April 3, 459

From Sparrow Mus, village of Kaaber, Scanra

I write in haste.

The people of my village are packing their things to flee.

Three days ago a group of warriors camped in our streets. They drank all the ale our small tavern had in its cellars and told the owner he should not complain because there would be no more travelers from the town to the south to drink it. They said, "The victory maidens ride the lightning for the new king of all Scanra."

As they roistered in the tavern, some children pulled the canvas off the wagon. They laid bare an iron monster 6 feet or so in height. Its limbs are an iron giant's bones moved by chains on wheels. The force that works them is some vile magic. I can smell it. I remind the Hostler that my Gift for smelling magic is why I was placed here.

The fingers and toes of the thing are blades. The head is a bowl with no neck.

The children screamed when they saw the thing, but it did not move. I ran to push them away from the wagon.

I did not move them soon enough. The warriors returned and struck them and me with the flats of their swords while more covered the thing with its canvas again.

Their leader made all of the villagers come to stand by the wagon. "A word to anyone," he told us, "and we do to this place what we just did to that other town, understand."

We understood. Now they are gone and the people are leaving. No one wants to wait to see if that warrior changes his mind and sends his killing device to finish us off. I will send word of my next placement when I find a proper courier.

—Mus

Note to the Chancellor and Whisper Man by Harvester Scalzin:

Given the date and the placement of Mus's village, I am certain the attack made by these warriors and their monster was that on the village of Slywater, found but a day ago. Only 3 inhabitants among 37 were found alive. The only one in the village when the attack began babbled of a giant insect that slew the people. The other 2 were hunting and did not see who murdered the others and burned the place.

Captain Jonnajin. I took this down as spoken

Report of contact with enemy forces near the Scanran border in patrol area designated to Fief Tirrsmont

Captain Narmon Jonnajin, 8th Mountain Regulars, in command, personally recording the report by Sergeant Fairburn Tennant, Company 3, 8th Mountain Regulars

Tennant reported:
Sir, I led Squad Green this morning, Corporal Whittle being sick with the liquid—well, sir, he'd had some bad meat last night, I think, so I took his squad and two extra women from my squad out—searchers, my folk were. Twelve soldiers in all, and that mage that calls himself Red Seeker. Fulk and Bendbow had the advance. I put my girls, Prout and Gress, on the right and left flank. Whittle's lads Moody and Westcot had our rear. We were on foot, coming up on the fishing village on the river, Whitewater. By the time we reached the water, it was dawn.

Our plan was to wait till the local men were out fishing for the day, then hit the village whilst the women were at their chores. We wanted a look in the barns. As you said when you briefed the company last night, sir, some of these local villages are dealing with the Scanrans, not just in goods, but turning a blind eye to warriors and mages. I'd a notion this village, Whitewater, was one of them.

We were in the wood by the riverbank when those pig anuses Fulk and Bendbow walked us right into a Scanran raiding party. I thought certain we could beat the mush out of them. When were a lot of Scanran screamers a match for Tortallan soldiers, strong and true?

Forgive me, sir. Might I have a moment? Forgive me.

Yes, yessir, the healers think Gress will live. No promises if she'll be able to fight again, of course. She doesn't know Prout and Westcot are gone. I'll have to tell her that, when she can bear it. Or about the others.

Yes, sir. Thank you, sir.

Red Seeker laid down curtains of flame, sir. He trapped them right there on the riverbank. I was that proud of him. Them Scanrans was jumping into the river to get away from the fire, and of course the current there is just vile.

But some of them ran for a thing on the riverbank, all bundled up in canvas. They hacked the cloth open, and I recall one of them saying something, words, but not Scanran. I speak that tongue well, even some of the dialects, they call them. It wasn't anything like Scanran.

A thing got up, sir, just like I told you before. I thought first it was an ogre of some kind, and I yelled for the squad to form up with me. They obeyed. I told you they're the best girls and boys in the realm. Any others might have run, but not them.

The Scanrans fought, they're the hardest warriors I know, but they only engaged our people when we tried to get around behind their monster. It was their thing, but they wouldn't go within ten feet of it. They was terrified of it. Mithros, I was terrified, but I knew we'd be dead if we turned our backs on it.

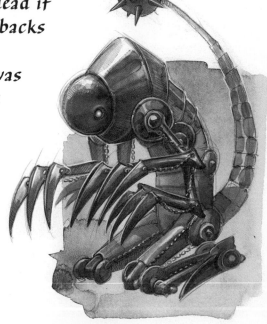

The thing was near seven feet tall, made of iron shaped like giant's bones. There was thin chains and rods attached to the elbows, shoulders, and wrists, then thin chains to the fingers. The same on the legs, chains and rods to the hips, the knees and the ankles, then thin chains to the blades they used for toes. It had blades for fingers, too, and those blades could gut a man. There were two elbows on both arms, and two knees on both legs, making them look spiderlike, almost. The head was like an upside-down bowl, all rough iron, with deep-set red glowing eyes, like coals from a fire. There were dagger teeth in the mouth. It ripped through my man Cassel with those teeth. There wasn't a gap between the monster's shoulders and head, or we might have pried the head off.

And it was fast, great Mithros save me, it was fast. Me and Lind, the biggest of the squad, we charged it, tried to shove it down the riverbank. I got inside those arms, but it cut me up, lifted me, and threw me. I got all these cursed slashes from that. It killed Lind and went after the others.

How many do I have left? Three, and that's if Byhan lives through the night. Red Seeker died on the march back. All four of us that's left are wounded bad. My army life is over. I'll never do a long march on this leg again. A fine squad, and that thing turned us to catmeat.

And you say that raiding party went on to Slywater village, killed most of the folk, and took the survivors back into Scanra. What the pox are they going to do with them? They can scarce feed themselves over there, along the river. How will they feed our people?

Apologies, sir. I'm not used to failing.

End report.

Signed in my own hand,

Fairburn Tennant, Sergeant

Witnessed by

Narmon Jonnajin, Captain

April 25, 459

His Majesty, King Jonathan of Conté

To Sergeant Fairburn Tennant, Company 3,
8th Mountain Regulars

Copy to Captain Narmon Jonnajin, 8th Mountain
Regulars, in command

Sergeant Tennant,

Your report was passed on to us through
emergency channels. You and your patrol
were not the only ones to find such a metal
monster, though your people paid the highest
price to date.

You have our solemn vow, both Her
Majesty's and mine, that your people will
not go unavenged. Your injuries will not go
unavenged. Troops, knights, and mages are
gathering even now to report to the Scanran
border to face whatever is coming to us from
our newest enemies to the north.

And you may yet serve, if you will,
as may your fellow survivors. We need
you soldiers who have lived through this
encounter to tell the new troops and their
officers what you saw. If you can bring

yourself to remain on the border to advise and to serve your next commanding officer as a clerk, we shall promise that your family will not want. The same is true for your fellow advisors.

Your dead will not be forgotten, Sergeant, whatever your decision.

Signed under my own seal,

Jonathan, King

Copy of document with note to John Juggler

From Deputy Nursemaid Fallow Deer

April 26, 459

My apologies for the copy of this letter,
but the original had His Majesty's original
signature and his seal by the time I saw it. I
felt I could do no better than to make a copy.
He has already summoned three generals and
the captains of two units of the King's Own,
as well as the Knight Commander of the
King's Own, to his study, where he and Her
Majesty spoke with them for several hours.
He has sent for members of the treasury this
morning, but I must send this out to you.
I shall try to listen to those conversations,
but it is very difficult to eavesdrop on His
Majesty. He has an ugly tendency to raise
spells that alert him to any spies.

Fallow Deer

How Lord Sir Wyldon of Cavall Became Training Master

12 April, 442

To Lord Sir Wyldon of Cavall,
from King Jonathan IV, greetings.

I hope the spring, new and rainy as it is, treats
you kindly in Cavall. When last we spoke, over
the Midwinter holiday, you mentioned that this
was a crucial year for your deerhound lines; I look
forward to the new generation, which, I imagine, is
just finding its voice in the kennels.

Earlier this week, Duke Gareth and I discussed
his approaching retirement as training master. I am,
of course, reluctant to let him go, but the realm
can hardly ask for more than he has given. We had
addressed the question of a new training master
at the last session of the Council of Lords, and
your name was foremost. Your record of service is
upstanding in every way, and those squires who
worked in your service have become the finest of
knights. We would be most pleased to see you take
those noble youths seeking knighthood in hand,
and Duke Gareth is in agreement. I believe his
words were, "If it is rigor you seek, you will not
find better than Wyldon of Cavall."

We await your thoughts, and welcome any
questions, on the matter. Please tender my warmest
regards to Lady Vivenne and your daughters.

Jonathan IV

To His Majesty King Jonathan of Conté,
from Lord Wyldon of Cavall, greetings.

His Majesty is gracious to ask; the
rains have not caused more damage than
Cavall has seen in years previous. The
work done to improve drainage in the fields
has kept our topsoil from being swept
away in the ongoing downpour. My Lady
and daughters are well, though restless
at the weather. They are honored by your
remembrance.

As concerns the dogs, we've not lost a
single one this year. The runt has taken a
liking to my daughter Eiralys that seems
more unshakable the closer the pups come
to weaning age. His Majesty would be
welcome to select from among those of the
new generation deemed fit for the hunt.

I am honored by such high
recommendations, and at the consideration
of my appointment to the position of
training master. It would indeed be
difficult to step into a post so long and
superbly filled. Nothing can be said of
Duke Gareth if not that he produced some
of the finest young fighting men Tortall
has seen in generations. They served with

honor in war and rebellion, and Mithros grant will continue to serve until age or injury prevents it.

The appointment itself is one I must consider with care. I know you will understand if I do not immediately consent. There is, after all, the matter of Cavall's operation in my absence. While my Lady is more than capable, it would be unwise to depart without thorough provisions being made. Likewise, I must consider the concerns of my associates who stay closer to court than myself. There are affairs of state that bring them some discomfort, which, if I were to accept, would seem to matter little to me. This is not the case.

I pray you will have patience as I weigh the generosity of Your Majesty's offer against the duties of friendship and Cavall's affairs.

Yours in fealty,

Lord Sir Wyldon of Cavall

17 April, 442

To Lord Sir Wyldon of Cavall,
from King Jonathan IV, greetings.

I am very glad to hear that your new
drainage is helping; we had reports of some
inlets jumping their banks. All pray for the
rains to abate and return next year in milder
humor—it is a pity indeed for the ladies to be
confined indoors.

I will speak to the Mistress of Hounds—I
believe you have met her, Jessamine Leris—about
visiting Cavall to look over the pups. It would
be good to have a Cavall deerhound again after
old Willow's passing. If I did not mention it
at Midwinter, I must say that the wolfhounds
were splendid over the winter—littermates out
of your Fallon, if I recall correctly, three or
four years ago.

I respect your desire to think our offer
through. It was my hope that, raising your
name and writing you that day, we would have
time to discuss the appointment before the
harvest demands your attention—but I have
no doubts all will go smoothly. Many at court
would be glad to see you here in an abiding
capacity. Though your time would be much
taken up with the pages, I do not doubt your
friends would value your voice being added to

their own, in whatever ways attend those bonds of friendship. The dues go both ways, surely. No true friend would wish you to turn down the appointment on his behalf, nor go to an appointment unwillingly; no more do I.

Jonathan IV

To Lord Sir Wyldon of Cavall, greetings.

It has been too long. I hope all continues well at Cavall, as it was when last we spoke. Leor of Seabeth also sends his regards—he and I recently watched a demonstration bout together, and I mentioned I would be writing you. The philosophical difference that day was of some interest all around, concerning as it did the longsword techniques coming across the Drell. Have you seen their work with half-swording, hooks, and traps? Benthan of Macayhill got a nasty surprise: his Tusaine opponent, Sir Cabe, reinforced a high-line parry as we might do, but where we would bind through, Cabe kept his left-handed grip on his blade and stepped in, tangling up the hilts to send Benthan's weapon clattering across the ring. Still in the half-sword grip, Cabe flipped his point up into Benthan's ribs and—but for a good evasion—would have added his elbow in the lad's face.

We frowned on that sort of thing in my day. Desperate measures at best.

The Shang teaching the pages hand-to-hand fighting should have inured me to surprise—how lately they were a mystery. I report with great satisfaction that Benthan rallied and took the Tusaine two out of three.

His Majesty let me know that you are taking some time to consider the training master position, as is only appropriate. We cannot, we must not, compel you—the gods know the only thing that could make the job harder is if you are fighting it—but our neighbors' eyes are on us, always. Our strength is in these young men—or, rather, it will be. For their offer of service, we owe them the most exacting, the most thoughtful training we can give them, to make them new knights for these new times. I do not mean to school you in chivalry—that time is long past between us. What I want, rather, is to lend weight to my final lines: I feel it is time for me to retire. I hope you see fit to take my place.

Duke Gareth of Naxen

To His Grace Duke Gareth of Naxen, greetings.

I had heard something about the match, but no such details. Indeed, I would hope the majority would still frown upon such graceless and reckless practices, though I do and will always say that knowledge of popular tactics and measures against them can be the line that divides the living from the dead.

I wonder perhaps if this youthful interest stems from the study of Shang fighting techniques. A change in martial education can sometimes lead to a shift in code, both of honor and morals. I do not by any means deny that the Shang Dragon should be honored for his heroic death. The study of his school of fighting is a most appropriate tribute. It is true that Shang as a means of combat has its uses. Its warriors are often beyond reproach, but their education is not one bound by duty and chivalry. With each additional sphere of influence to which we expose our future knights, the cementing of traditional principles becomes that much more important.

But I stray from the point of our discourse. You wish for me to take up your mantle. I am moved by your request. I will inform *His Majesty* of my acceptance forthwith. An invitation from a king is one kind of honor, the appeal of a mentor quite another.

Respectfully,

Wyldon of Cavall

24 April, 442

To His Majesty King Jonathan of Conté,
from Lord Wyldon of Cavall, greetings.

I hope this missive finds you well.
I will not dally on pleasantries. If I
am to take up the position of training
master, I would like to begin discussing
the transfer of duties and potential
alterations to both the page training
schedule and the educations of squires
beyond the responsibilities given by
their knight-masters. I am coming to
Corus to begin arrangements, with your
permission, and plan to pay my respects
to Seneschal Evret of Jonnajin as I
pass through Conté. I will give him your
regards.

Yours in fealty,

Lord Sir Wyldon of Cavall

27 April, 442

To Lord Wyldon of Cavall,
from King Jonathan IV, greetings.

I take your letter to mean you have
accepted the position; we are honored and
look forward to hearing your plans in more
detail. Send word when you arrive in Corus,
and we will invite you and Duke Gareth to
dine with us.

Jonathan IV

24 April, 422

To Remic of Princehold,
from Lord Sir Wyldon of Cavall, greetings.

I am writing to reopen the discourse
we began when last I was in Corus. I do
not know how swiftly rumor travels in the
capital. I make a point of not knowing.
Perhaps you have heard of the recent offer
that was made me. I have accepted the
position of training master for the pages
and plan to institute secondary education
for the squires.

This may surprise you, given my
objections to the royal proclamation
regarding the participation of females in
the institution of knighthood. It is in part
for that reason that I agreed to the post.
Who better than the training master to
protest, should the proclamation lead to
a swarm of adventurous girls declaring
themselves the revival of the woman
knights of old? I know we discussed in
brief the measures that might be taken
to repeal or overturn the proclamation in
court. I would like to extend the research
of our options and begin to prepare the

documentation necessary to take the
matter to the magistrates.

If it is agreeable, I shall send you a
retainer's fee to this end. Please write
to me at the palace with your estimated
expenses and judicial costs. I will send
you whatever funds you need.

Mithros bless,

Lord Sir Wyldon of Cavall

Immortals

June 30, 447

Kourrem Hariq to the Whisper Man

From the village of Deepwater,
the north border of Fief Dewain

For the last ten days I have been watching
a family of unicorns. They number a sire, dam,
filly, and colt.

Laugh if you must. What else do you call
long-maned, long-tailed horses with coats that
shimmer, pearl-like hooves, and a long, twisting
horn in the center of their foreheads?

These are solid in color. The sire is fire
chestnut, the dam black. Both young ones are
a light brown that blends with the land and
foliage here. The horns are real. The unicorns
are real. I have tested both, gently, with my
spells. I got knowledge of their reality and a
wicked headache thereby.

They aren't the sweet, affectionate unicorns
of the pale-skinned people's tales and ballads,
either. A lout of a trapper stumbled across the

filly and colt yesterday. The parents kicked him to death, then trampled him to paste. I stay well back and downwind as I follow them.

Yesterday a hollow circle of magic opened ahead of them. They walked into it. It closed, and they were gone.

Have you knowledge of anything like this? We mages need to know if you do!

KOURREM, drinking a calming tea

August 30, 447 H.E.

To George, Baron of Pirate's Swoop
From Coram, Baron of Trebond

George, do you know what my little
Jonthair said to me this morning? "Da," he
says, "there's people with metal wings instead
of arms, and claws instead of legs, sitting
on the observing tower. And they don't have
clothes, not even the ladies." It's usually
Alinna that's the tale spinner.

I said, "How did they get up there?"

"From a big fire in the air," Jonthair says,
like all guests come that way. "Da, they're
going to get cold." Behind him I see Alinna
and Thomsen run by with half the linen closet
in their arms.

I follow my children to our observation
tower and there they are. Seven great things,
flapping off into a burning hole in the sky.
They had steel feathers and claws, from what
I could see and confirm later, human heads
and chests, long hair with ribbons in it. When
one cheeky nasty monster turns to grin at us,
I see sharp steel teeth! And my children are
jumping and waving and calling these things
to come back!

One left a feather
behind. I'm sending this
rubbing to you. That's
how I know their feathers
are steel, and how you'll
know I haven't been
broaching the mead more
than I should.

What are they,
George? Why has there
been no word of them?
What do all my taxes
pay for if monsters with
daggers for teeth can
land atop my castle and
charm my little ones
into giving away my
shirts? Not to mention
leave a stink behind
them that took three
rounds of scrubbing to
get out of the stones!

I know my tales, Master Whisper Man.
Anything even a little like those creatures
went into the Realms of the Gods ages ago.
Will you be telling me why we saw one here?

Coram
Baron of Trebond

To Lord Harailt of Aili
Head of the Tortallan University and Dean
of Magical Studies

With copies to the Heads of Academic
and Healing Studies

From Nealan of Queenscove

4th day of February, 452

Sir,

I am writing to formally declare my
intent to withdraw from my studies
at the University. As you know, both
of my older brothers were killed in the
strange immortal attacks that took place
over the winter, and I find myself quite
suddenly the Queenscove heir. It is an
honor I never expected, and comes with
responsibilities I had not previously
considered. Queenscoves have always
served the throne as knights—twelve, all
told—and with Graeme and Cathal on the
rolls I felt free to pursue magecraft. But
now it falls to me to uphold tradition,

and do my duty to my house, by earning a knight's shield. My father allows it is my right to make this choice, and I await only your response before petitioning the Crown. I hope you will understand and approve this course of action; please know that in ordinary times, nothing could drag or drive me away from this place of learning.

I remain respectfully yours,

Nealan of Queenscove

Daine's Immortals Notes

Basilisk—Friendly, curious folk. Academics who don't much like fighting. Built like lizards—they get up over seven feet when on their hind legs, easily. They have pebbled skin, like beading, not scales. All I've seen have been gray or bluish. Slit pupils. They have a belly pouch where they carry their young or store things. They're no threat to humans who leave them alone. They eat rocks, all sorts, with precious stones being considered delicacies like human sweets.

Related to dragons and wyverns. They're good for translation and as ambassadors, being as they speak all mortal and divine languages from when they're young. They speak mind to mind, too. Those newly from the Divine Realms talk mind to mind until they know how to speak aloud. They feel great magics being worked and walk through even the most powerful magical barriers. Human magic does very little to them. They turn creatures to stone with a whistled spell that never fails, ever, though Numair can break free of it given the chance. They also call light to stones and can find particular types of rock, which makes them popular mine workers.

Centaur—Human upper half, horse lower half. All sorts of colors. There's two kinds of centaurs—the peaceful sort and the blood-hungry. Peaceful centaurs have hooves and hands. The bloodthirsty have fangs, talons in place of hooves, and fingers tipped with claws.

Youth lasts two centuries, but they never age past adulthood. Centaurs have a spoken language that horses understand. Centaur women attack and abandon stallions who don't give them gifts. It makes them either good trading partners or bad bandits.

They call horses slaves. Herdmasters view humans as worth only a bit more than horses. Raoul's former squire, the Lady Knight Keladry? He said a herdmaster offered three horses for her in trade because she was a fine strong female who'd birth plenty more centaurs. Human women are able to birth a centaur child, but it most often kills them, if carrying the child doesn't do it first.

Herdmasters cull troublemaking members of their herd. They kill the horses that bred with the troublemakers, to make sure they've stamped out the bad blood. The centaur goddesses of vengeance are the Mares with Bloody Teeth. They take blood sacrifices and the leavings of the culled. Most centaurs are open to treaties with humans if the treaties are fair.

Centaurs fight with both handheld weapons and

their horse parts, using their horse parts like a trained warhorse, though their tricks are more sophisticated. There's a vulnerable spot where the horse and human parts meet. The Lady Knight Keladry says a strike in that spot seems akin to kicking a man between his legs.

They use the longbow as a distance weapon and their arrows are ofttimes fletched with the feathers of other immortals. They scorn crossbows. They have a dog's sense of smell—though the tricks folks use to duck scent hounds work on them, too.

Centaurs hide their passage and their presence with magic, same as other immortals do. When they hide, they don't show in scrying crystals or other magical means. Human mages can use a hair from a centaur's tail to force the centaur's obedience, but centaurs have mages of their own, and they don't take well to being forced into service.

Dragon—Arrogant as anything. They're the scholars of the Divine Realms. They have long, delicate-looking bodies, scaled like a reptile's, with bat wings that are lit up by their bones. Their claws, teeth, and bones are all a soft silver color. They have slit-pupiled eyes like a cat's. They come in all colors, from black and white to bright red. They have crests, almost like a lizard's. The crests aren't sensitive. More like scale or bone. The edges of their scales are razor-sharp and can't be penetrated by any ordinary weaponry. It takes something like an immortal's claws to cut through.

Dragonets aren't much bigger than a large cat, though their teeth are as sharp as an adult's. Newborn are soft. Their scales haven't had time to harden, which makes them vulnerable to attack. In their infancy, which lasts about three years, they get to be around two feet long with an extra foot or so of tail. The young dragons in the Divine Realms, two and three hundred years old respectively, were about six to eight feet long from nose to tail tip. By mid-adolescence (which they reach after ten centuries), they get to be around fifteen to twenty feet long. Seemingly they grow about two feet every one hundred years. Adults get to be hundreds of feet long.

They're extremely good with magic and aren't much affected by human spells. Even at a young age they understand human speech and the mind-speech of other immortals. They don't gain the ability to mind-speak themselves until they're about ten years old, but they're born knowing the spoken dragon language. Even the youngest dragons are very intelligent and curious. Kitten followed what was going on in the negotiations with Ozorne, and she was barely more than an infant then.

Their home in the Divine Realms is called the Dragonlands. It's bordered on one side by Stormwing Eyries and on the other by the Sea of Sand. The border is marked by fire. They agreed long ago to ban visiting the Mortal Realm, even though the barriers that seal the Divine Realms couldn't stop dragons. They've been cut off from mortals for so long that most of

them don't really know what's going on in the Mortal
Realm, though they'd tell you otherwise.

They have a gathering called the Dragonmeet.
They get everyone together to argue over lawmaking
and other things. It's ruled over by the oldest of the
dragons. That was Rainbow when we were there.
They debate until a human could die of old age, and
they mightn't agree on anything even then. They're
academics and politicians in one scaly bundle, and
they don't like change. Some—the younger ones, or
those that keep a closer eye on things outside the
Dragonlands—are more amicable about bending the
rules. The Dragonmeet is what put a ban on visiting
the Mortal Realm. Dragons live in clans, though they
refer to each other as relatives no matter how distant
the relation.

They're "mages of the air," born with a natural
talent for magic. Even infant dragons unlock doors or

pop out locks with vocalizations, though Kitten is mor
advanced than her cousins. Dragons put out flames
with a sound, call light to stones or their scales, and
do all sorts of small spells with whistles. They use
their magic for practically anything. They cast fire
from their forepaws. Adults summon fire with a snarl.
Invisibility spells are useless against them, and they
see other spells. They're able to put a spell of silence
on someone, binding a victim's mouth shut. Human
spells just wash off adult dragons like nothing. Their
magic lets them see things that mortals don't sense at
all, even the presence of gods and god-born children.
Nothing hides from a dragon. An adult dragon, it's
said, is powerful enough to do battle with a god.

Dragons change color to suit their mood or to show
when they're feeling a strong emotion. They turn pink
when they're scared and red when they're angry. When
they're really angry, they scorch the ground under their
paws without meaning to. Lightning flickers over their
hides, getting thicker the madder they are.

They travel within a realm by vanishing from one
location and appearing almost at once where they want
to go. They can send others away using the same
skill. They go where they like, and unlike all other
immortals, they're able to carry others with them when
they travel between realms. Even the gods can't refuse
a dragon passage. The spell to travel between realms
is called a spiral spell and involves flying up into
the clouds and then back down in a corkscrew flight

pattern. Young dragons can't do it—even at three centuries, their wings aren't able to carry them. Once they can fly, though, they maneuver like swifts and are incredibly fast.

No mortal or immortal senses the magic of a dragon being worked. Their invisibility spells are better than any human spell, masking the sight, sound, and smell of them. The only telltale sign of an invisible dragon is a bit of bending in the light when they move. Dragons can't hide from each other, and if you're close enough to touch a dragon, you see as the dragon does.

They're no threat to humans, not as things stand. We'd learn far more from them than maybe any other immortal. If we could get them to teach us.

Griffin —Large, feathered cats, with the head, beak, and wings of an eagle. Males are only a little bigger than females, most griffins being around five to seven feet tall at the shoulder. You tell their sex the same way you do a cat's. Their claws are as long as my forearm. They're intelligent. They speak in ideas and feelings instead of words. Human voices grate on them and they don't trust us, so they usually nest in places we can't reach. They warn us off their nests if we live close by. Most have coloring that's either raptor colors or bright, metallic shades. Sometimes you'll see griffins with both. Most often their eyes are a similar color to their feathers. Griffin voices run through cat and raptor noises—squawks, screeches, chirps, hisses,

growls, and yowls. That said, you won't mistake them for a bird or a cat.

They're not a threat to humans, so long as humans leave them alone. When angered or threatened, griffins hunch up their shoulders, spread their wings, and lower their heads like some birds of prey do when protecting a kill. Infant griffins beg for food like bab birds, fluttering their wings and opening their beaks for a meal.

Most griffins live a short flight from the coast or from big lakes. A lot of them nest in the Copper Isles. They eat dolphins, seals, sea lions, and the like, but mostly fish. They don't like grass-eaters. Sheep and pigs and such. They have to clean themselves, preenin and licking, to keep their feathers healthy. Young griffins usually learn to fly short distances within their first year. Babies sense their parents nearby the same way adults sense their young.

Folks who trade in live young are asking for death. If a griffin smells its offspring on a person, even year later, they'll kill that person, no question. The scent doesn't go away. Numair calls it a kind of magical residue, since it lasts so long. Only those who've handled a live griffin or any part of griffin bodies carry the scent in this way. Feathers or claws, things that griffins shed, those are harmless except for the risk of gathering them. Griffins won't tolerate being caged. They're able to rust metal into nothing. Ozorne had a griffin caged in that awful menagerie, but he had to keep it magicked and the cage was magic, too.

There's no telling a lie around a griffin. Griffin leather used to be popular for shields, because whatever makes it impossible to lie to a living griffin carries over to the hide. Griffin feathers are worth their weight in gold. Arrows fletched with them are mage-killers and never miss, flying true even through illusions. Coverings for the eyes and ears made out of griffin feathers dispel illusion magics. Numair learned about that from Lady Kel. Griffins know that humans value their feathers, and they distrust humans in part because of the way we use them for their truth-telling properties. Stealing their young, killing them for their hides, all of that. Numair said there used to be spells to trap baby griffins in "undeath." Folk would catch them, wait for them to fledge, and then use magic to sink them partway into shields. Not living. Not dead. No way to bring them back. The only people who die by a griffin's paws usually deserve it.

Hurrok—They're cousins to flying horses, with a name that started as "horse-hawk." Their wings are like bat wings, though. Not feathered, but webbed, with silver bones like long fingers and a claw at the tip of the "thumb" bone. They've predator's fangs, forward-set eyes, and talons instead of hooves. They have the same coloring as regular horses.

They're intelligent and capable of mind-speech with wildmages, horses, centaurs, and other winged

creatures. They live like horse herds. Several small, related groups make up a single herd, each herd being led by a mare. Most males are driven out when they mature. They often fly together until they find mares of their own and establish a new herd. Their verbal communication is more like raptors than horses. They shriek, scream, and shrill. They're flesh-eaters and hunt like raptors, diving for prey talons-first. They're not invulnerable. They're naturally violent and wrathful. Slavery only makes that worse. It's best to avoid engaging with them.

Merfolk — You can tell at a glance that they aren't human. They're fully scaled from the hips down, with flesh blending to scales around the navel. Even in their skin you see scale patterns. There are as many colors of merfolk as there are fish in the sea and their scales are

like fish scales, too. Their teeth are sharp and as tough as immortal claws. Little ones tend to be about the same size and weight as a human four-year-old. Bull males get to be over seven feet in length, and females are usually five and a half or six feet long. Some travel on the backs of tamed porpoises, tuna, grouper, or dolphins. Their warriors ride sharks.

They wear skirts and loincloths to cover their genitals. The women wear wrap scarves, and all merfolk like to wear decorative vests or armlets, sleeveless clothes, and armbands. They like pretty things, almost as much as crows, which is the only reason they started talking to humans. They only deal with folk they trust, most of those being sailors or people from seaside towns. If you betray them or let them down just once, they won't trust you again. It's best to avoid ever going to sea if you've betrayed one of the merfolk. They don't forget.

They've their own mages, doctors, merchants, and scholars. For a price, they'll help bring up shipwrecks, trade in deep-sea fish and treasures, and work to guide fleets and navies safe across the ocean. Most sailors have a healthy respect for them, as merfolk sense the presence of whales, heavy storms, and the kraken. For the right price, they'll work with fleets or serve as couriers.

Since it's as hard for them to bear young as it is for most immortals, they like mortal children. Never fear that they'll hurt a child. Even a merman with a grudge would never. They'll take children for rides on the sea, play with them on the beaches, and bring them toys from their own craftsmen. They care a great deal about family and are very protective of their own children. Their pregnancies are slow, and their children's youths are long. Their nurseries are in underwater caves, well hidden and guarded from those who murder merfolk for their tail skin and meat. If your stomach turns at the idea the way mine does, keep in mind it's fair popular.

Merfolk refer to whales as sea slugs. Whales despise them as a lower form of animal. I suppose it's a comfort to know that whales are like that with everyone, though there are some merfolk and some whales that get along. They're oddities and often mocked for their association with enemies.

Ogre—They're

everywhere. They're a good deal tougher than we are, with heights varying from five to twelve feet. Nine feet is about average. Their hair is thin and grows from their foreheads as low as their neck and shoulders in back. They're aqua-skinned, with pointed ears that swivel, large peggish

teeth, and big eyes. Most times when ogres fight with humans, it's because the ogres are trying to take by force what belongs to others, not knowing there are rules or laws against doing so. Mainly, ogres are peaceful and prefer farming, building, and craftsmanship to fighting, though there are always a few in any given place that have a taste for battle and blood.

They're inventive and smart in most every craft they tackle: mining, smithcraft, fishing, glassmaking, pottery, weaving. They're the craftsmen of the Divine Realms. Ogres produce the best work in the world, though they prefer practical designs to things that are pretty for pretty's sake.

Ogres are very strong. Even small ones can lift huge loads with ease or shatter tree trunks with one blow. They have an odd understanding of plants, from millet plants to them as are used for dye.

The most famous ogre colony in Tortall is in Fief Dunlath. It's overseen by Lady Maura of Dunlath and the ogre Iakoju. The farms stretch from one end of the valley to the other, alongside the opal mines. Lords send their farmers and overseers from all around Tortall and our neighbors to learn from them, miners come to learn about mining, and mages come to study how the ogres deal with plants. Dunlath's become the center of Tortallan farming and opal mining thanks to the ogres.

Spidren—Spider-bodied, human-headed nightmares. About five feet from rump to crown. Their teeth are

sharp, a predator's teeth. They're furry, the females being mottled and the males black. Their spinneret is a light-colored shaft at the base of their bodies that shows when they rear up on their back legs to shoot web. They use tools and weapons and build fires, though they don't cook their meals. Spidren claws snip through their own webs easily—the claws on their legs are vicious sharp. Even their blood is dangerous. It's black and burns like acid.

They live in family groups. Their young put up a fight if they're attacked, but they're only about a foot or so tall. The biggest worry with spidren hatchlings is being mobbed, as a family of spidrens often has more than thirty eggs at once. (I'm told spidren young have to be taught to be savage. I'll believe it when I see it.) They don't have the problems reproducing that other immortals do.

Fortunately, they don't have any real defenses against regular human weapons.

Spidrens feed on blood, their favorite being human blood. They refuse to make any kind of peace with human beings. They usually take their prey home, biting off a limb or two and then binding the wound up with webbing so their victim won't die right off. The webbing seems to keep out infection, too, based on the health of some saved from spidrens. They like others' pain. The territories that attract them have a lot of trees and bare rock—woods and hill country. They vocalize with screams and keening noises when they're angry, but they speak human languages, and they talk to each other in human tongues.

Spidrens hunt in all manner of ways. They make web traps and hide them under sand, leaves, or other debris. These traps shift to hold a creature no matter its size. They hang web between trees to catch flying things and riders on horseback, but it can be seen, especially in the dark. They also shoot web across water and then reel in whatever gets stuck, like a fisherman with a line. Spidrens swim.

Fresh, ordinary web is gray or gray-green, as thick as good rope. It floats. When it's fresh, it sticks like tar. Impossible to get off unless you scrape it away with blades or sprinkle it with powders we've made that dissolve it. Pink web burns living flesh and leaves welts where it hits. All web glows yellow-green in the dark.

The beasts shoot web ten feet or more, using it to climb cliffsides or trees as well as trap prey. When a trapmaker or a web spinner gets killed, their web turns liquid and dissolves. They have a small amount of magic, spells that shield them, which makes it hard for mages to track them or for any talismans or charms to warn of spidren presence. Human travelers have died from trusting faulty charms in spidren territory.

Animals sense them. Even the steadiest of the People goes near mad with fear when spidrens are around. Big animals flee, and small animals hide. Dogs won't hunt spidrens unless they've been specially trained. It takes days for animals to come back to a place after the spidrens are gone.

Stormwing—Human heads and chests, with an immense hawk's lower body, wings, and talons. They have sharp teeth. Their bird parts are fashioned from bright steel, though they look exactly like bird parts otherwise. Their feathers are beautiful but razor sharp. They look as different from each other as humans do, and they have their own view of what's pretty. Feathers, bones. They wear things braided into their hair, sometimes necklaces or other bobbles, put on with the help of magic. They smell dreadful. They're always covered in filth and nastiness from the battlefield— you've seen enough of their ways now to know. They see like hawks, very good long-distance vision, but there's nothing magical about it.

They dine on human fear and anger. They empty their bowels on the bodies of them that fall in battle, then roll around in it when they're finished. They can go without a meal for centuries, but they don't like it. Other immortals sometimes call them Eaters.

They have a hard time flying low or in close quarters. They can't change direction fast. They're built to fly, and they can't walk properly on their talons. They have to hop. It's undignified as anything. It's hard for them to take off from flat ground once they've landed. That said, they stay aloft for days with the barest help of magic. Tumbling from up high is

dangerous—their wings oftentimes cut them to pieces when they hit ground. Those same wings are better than armor when it comes to deflecting arrows. Their feathered parts can't be hurt, and they cut you if you touch them. Infections from Stormwing feathers are bad, very bad. Their talons cut stone easily.

Their magic isn't unlike ours. They have a thing called War Terror, fear that they force on their opponents. You fight it off the same way you fight through ordinary fear—willpower and stubbornness. Stormwings conjure up bolts of gold fire by pointing a claw, they scry as humans do, and they can see a mage's spirit when it's outside of the mage's body. (Spirit projection, Numair calls it.) Human mages see Stormwing magic easily if they know what they're looking for. The aura of it shows for miles, and when Stormwings work magic, it appears scarlet and gold. Any complicated spells need to be spoken aloud in the Stormwing language.

They pass through most magical barriers without much effort. They're drawn to places of strife when they sense there's fighting on the horizon. Sometimes they help by joining one side or the other. Not all Stormwings, but some enjoy stirring humans up.

If a human drives a Stormwing feather into their arm, they turn into a Stormwing. No changing back. Stormwings are vulnerable to human magic, but they shield themselves against it, too. The best remedy for an attacking Stormwing is an arrow in the throat, though the scent of onions is as nasty to them as Stormwing stink is to us. Numair's onion bombs send them packing.

They nest like large seabirds, in eyries made up of nations, as they call them. Their eyries in the Divine Realms border along the Dragonlands. Each nation is led by a king or queen or both, and consorts are known as lords and ladies. They have their own customs, their own laws, and their own forms of justice. When challenging a Stormwing king or queen for the crown, it's dishonorable to attack from behind or without warning. Formal challenges mean one-on-one combat to the death. Breaches of honor and tradition are very grave. If you lie about it, that only makes things worse. They value noble enemies and take being indebted to others very seriously. At least those who believe in honor and tradition do. They hold grudges for a very, very long time.

Stormwings were dreamed by a woman traveler ages ago. She tired of the waste of death and the leavings of war. She dreamed of a creature that would make war so ugly that folk would balk at sending their children off to fight. Them that make offerings to buy Stormwings off are them that get defiled first.

They're temperamental and proud, but they're not heartless nor evil. They won't seek refugees, though they'll go after the dead around armed camps. And they don't touch the bodies of folk that died without fighting. It's hard for Stormwings to have children of their own—they're born from steel eggs that oftentimes kill the mother Stormwing who carries it, before it's ever laid. They have a soft spot for the young. They've been known to save them from riots and attacks, and they look after neglected human children.

It's comfortable to think that they're just monsters. But they're thinking, reasoning, and feeling creatures, with their own beliefs and loyalties. Their nature makes them repulsive to us, but we're repulsive to them. We kill more of our own than they ever kill of their kind. They scorn mortals, almost all mortals, even the People, but humans in particular. It's just the way they are. The ones that take a liking to us are called soft and a lot worse. Stormwings are stubborn in their ways. Their nature is opposed to ours. That doesn't mean they're without reason. They can even be friendly, in their own way.

Tauros — These are only male. They were born from women's fear of rape. I told my da it was wrong that they were without women of their own kind. He told the Great Gods, who said there was nothing they could do. According to Mithros, it's against the nature of tauroses' being for females of their kind to exist, because of why they came to be. The gods did confine the tauros to the Divine Realms. The things don't reproduce. Their victims don't live. A woman caught by a tauros gets ripped to pieces. According to my da, as long as rape exists, the tauros will, too.

They're stupid. They can't communicate with us but have their own way of talking to each other. They're seven feet tall, with short, thick horns, a bull neck and broad shoulders, with a predator's front-facing eyes. Their noses are more human, but flat and squarish, and their teeth look almost too big for their jaws. Their bodies are manlike, built big enough to support the bull head. They also have hairy legs with splayed hooves, ox tails, and a ridged spine, bad eyesight and a very good sense of smell. They find their victims by scent. Their blood is silver. They can be killed by ordinary weapons.

<u>Unicorn</u>—They don't like the cold, so they stick
to warmer regions. There are deer-sized unicorns,
boarhound-sized unicorns, and cat-sized unicorns.
Often you find the peaceful unicorns in the company
of deer herds, partly as camouflage and partly to stay
warm. Both peaceful and killer live in abandoned
barns and outbuildings for the same reason. The killer
unicorns have fangs and claws as well as their horn.
All come in horse-ish colors.

Killer unicorns are hunters and meat-eaters. They
live alone with their mates and any young offspring.
They mate for life. The more peaceful sort live in
small herds related through sisterhood. They're grazers,
herbivores, and have multiple mates. Both kinds foal
easily, as the horn develops after birth. A unicorn's

age shows in the turns of the horn. They shed the outer shell of their horns like male deer shedding antler velvet. Unicorns of either sort do not shed their horns entirely. Unicorn horns are more like elephant tusks than many deer antlers. They aren't for ornament. Other immortals have been found dead with injuries from a unicorn attack.

People hunt both sorts for their horns, though unicorns are protected by law. Even the discarded shell is valuable. Horns and horn shells strengthen magical workings. They also get sold as curiosities for the wealthy.

Unicorn hooves are incredibly sharp. They safeguard their young very well. If you come across a unicorn foal alone, be ready to run. Folk have died from being too close when a herd was around. Even a pair of small unicorns can put a human down. Grazing unicorns don't attack human children. They have rescued children in the wild and kept the child with the herd until they found other humans. Some folk use children as bait when hunting unicorns. Unicorn magic is so powerful that children turn on such hunters. Killer unicorns will not touch children, but they won't help them. They leave the area. Unicorns in captivity do not thrive.

Winged Ape—Fair clever folk. They mostly keep to themselves and build their villages high up in trees or on cliffsides. Sometimes on castle roofs if they find

a good place to nest. If you start finding big splats on your parapets, check for winged apes upstairs. Though they don't have fireplaces, they're better at proofing against snow, ice, and high wind than humans. Many winged apes live up at the Roof of the World.

They mate for life, but they canoodle a lot before they mate. They don't have much magic. They make fog, light, and a breeze, and can control when they get pregnant. Good fighters, weapon users, but vulnerable to human weapons and magic.

Winged apes like to trade with farming ogres, especially for meats or plants they can't grow high up. The apes are the best grape-growers and bee-tenders, producing the best wines and meads in the Eastern Lands. The winged apes at the Roof herd goats and yaks to make butters and fermented milks. They prefer to trade with other immortals than with humans. They turn mean if they're betrayed, and they don't forget or forgive. Them that served Ozorne were told that Tortallan humans stole them from the Divine Realms. They turned on Ozorne's people when they learned he lied.

Winged Horse—Mostly peaceful cousins to the

hurroks. The big ones mainly live in the Copper Isles, where they're sacred, though they are scattered lightly around the Eastern Lands, especially Sarain. They look like horses with big bat wings, though their bones are hollow like a bird's, and they come in horse colors with horse markings. There's three different kinds. The smallest are only about the size of a wildcat when full-grown. The middle ones get as big as wolfhounds. The biggest are horse-sized. The littlest like to live near farms so they can steal what they want, though they have to have help to carry off anything cabbage-sized or bigger. Humans try to catch them to keep as pets, but they're very fast and clever. They live in herds and have live births. They eat the same things that horses eat, but they don't get sick when they have too many treats. They love apples and carrots. The bigger kinds avoid humans. They only willingly come to descendants of the Copper Isles' original ruling line. Back when, it was one of their warrior queens who dreamed winged horses into being.

Wyvern —Lesser cousins to dragons. They have to obey when a dragon gives them an order. They fight it, but the bigger and older the dragon, the less luck the wyvern has. No legs and no arms. They're like snakes with wings, except their heads are more dragon

heads than snake heads. Their colors are like those of dragons. They're as smart as a young human child. Wyverns are big and hard to kill. They spit venom and breathe a yellow fog that burns human lungs and eyes. It causes long-lasting coughs and blurry vision. They shield themselves with magic. It's hard to see them and even harder to punch through their protection to injure them.

They prefer mountain caves, rocky heights, and cliff ledges. It's hard for wyverns to get pregnant, maybe because they like to mate in midair. They reach adulthood in a century and come in clutches of two or three eggs at a time. Not all hatch. Them that do are tended by adults until they can hunt for themselves.

Wyverns are predators. They eat deer, beaver, boar, sheep, cows, goats, whatever they're able to catch and carry. The ones that live near the sea eat seals, sea lions, dolphins, and any fish they get without diving too deep. They came flocking to the Mortal Realm because the gods consider them a delicacy. Can't hardly blame them, even if they are pests here.

They ride the wind. They sing beautifully. They lure prey to them that way. It's almost impossible to resist a wyvern's song. They have an odd sort of friendship with merfolk. When the two sing together, it's the most beautiful thing in the Realms. I got to hear merfolk singing with wyverns north of Blue Harbor once. I don't think I'll ever hear anything as lovely again.

In the words of Nightmane Longgallop,
Speaker for the centaur clans of the Drell Hills

May 18, 450

Your Majesties,

It is Nightmane here, the same Nightmane that bought safety for your merchants with the bows of the centaur clans when river pirates would have stripped them of their goods during the last full moon. Your merchants spoke much of their gratitude and gifted the clans with useful things. Your late-coming troops said the centaur clans of the hills had their gratitude. In trade for presents for our wives they have employed four of our young men as hunters and explorers.

Your letter with seals and ribbons of two weeks later said much the same. Gratitude blows on the wind and is gone with the autumn leaves. The centaurs of the Drell Hills have helped your travelers before. We could help them again, if we were not defending ourselves from hunting parties of young two-legger lords. They think us no more than animals.

If we are animals, Majesties of Tortall, why should we help your travelers when bandits and pirates prey upon them?

If we are not animals, why withhold our arrows from two-legged hunters? We belong to this realm or we do not, is it not so?

If it is so, the Drell Hills centaurs require a place in the councils that serve Your Majesties, as the lords and guilds and mages have a place. We require a voice in laws that are made to keep the wives and children safe. Is this not fair? Is it not reasonable between peoples of craft and virtue?

We await your answer, Majesties.

in the hand of Wedon Padric,
of Glassbrook village,
scribe to the speaker
for the Drell Hills centaurs

His Majesty and I are inclined to support speakers for the Drell Hills centaur and the Royal Forest centaur enclaves in the Royal Council and the Council of Mages, George. What do you think? Also it is our belief that if we grant places to the centaurs, it should be done for the ogre clans and merfolk rookeries.

Thayet

Advise Hostler Irhad: Need information with regard to Drell Hills centaurs: unity between clans had best be strong if we let one centaur speak for these eastern ones. Talk with this scribe, Wedon Padric in Glassbrook. Seemingly Nightmane trusts him with so unusual a document as this, so mayhap he trusts him with other things. Might Padric be worth bringing along as a Sparrow?

Copy to John Juggler with this note: Also contact Hostler Slowbrook and Harvester Crossways in the Royal Forest with regard to the centaur clans there. Might those clans wish to appoint a speaker for themselves united if it gives them a voice in the realm? It would also give us a way of learning how many clans are in the forest and where they're keeping themselves.

Similar poking about must be done for the merfolk and ogres, with no time wasted. —W.M.

Diplomat's Guide
to Tortall

June 20, 456

Most Honored Princess Shinkokami-sama,

   Once again, permit me to say what a pleasure
it has been for me to spend time with you,
talking about your coming marriage and your
forthcoming removal to my homeland. Truly
a foreigner could never hope for a warmer
welcome in the Islands than you have granted
to my family. Your courtesy and kindness eased
our longing for our home so much. We hope to
do the same for you when you arrive in Tortall.
   I am deeply honored that you have asked me
to write down for you some of the things we
have discussed about the differences between
life in Tortall and in the Islands. Your own
royal upbringing is such that your way will
be easier than that of many of your fellow
countrymen who come fresh to the Eastern
Lands, but I understand your concerns. Here
I will try to make note of what I feel will be
your chiefest strengths, the areas where you
may depend upon your Tortallan staff to assist
you, and the areas which would be pitfalls to
any foreign princess.

Also, please remember, you will not be left on your own. Lady Cythera of Naxen is to be your chief lady-in-waiting among the Tortallans. She is not only gracious and kind, but you will not find a lady more knowledgeable about the court, the palace, and their inner workings. Her husband, Sir Gareth the Younger of Naxen, is the king's right hand. No couple is better trusted by Their Majesties, and you may rely on them as you would on my husband and me. We will be at court for some months, at least until your marriage, and you may always call on us when you feel the need. We live to serve you. Your own Yamani ladies are devoted to you and they have a great deal of common sense. Also, at some point, you will encounter our youngest daughter, Squire Keladry of Mindelan. She belongs to your betrothed prince's group of friends. She will be delighted to see Your Highness again.

I have included a stuffy little pamphlet drawn up by the Royal Secretary of State's office as a guide to the realm. I think you will find it amusing—we can laugh about it when I join you on your voyage to Tortall. It rather usefully includes a map of the realm and of the capital. I could not help but notice that your own map is getting rather tattered, and mine is little better.

Conversation and gossip

While in the Islands it is considered acceptable
for a liege lord or lady to ask a vassal how many
horse warriors and infantry they may bring
to their lord's service, or how many barrels of
grain or other foodstuffs they harvest a year, as
this, too, is a matter of concern for their lord,
it is not considered polite to ask such things of
other lords and ladies in these lands. The lines
between overlords and vassals are far looser.
Subordinate nobles may volunteer information
along these lines, such as boasting about the
number of barrels of wine they put up in one
year, but the information is theirs to offer. The
king may ask for it, but not as conversation,
and he may not always get a truthful reply. The
view of the queen by many of his vassals is so
hostile that they would take her request for such
information with great hostility unless it was a
needful request for information in war.

Please do not ask if anyone has slaves.
Remember, no one in the Eastern Lands is
permitted to own them. Those people you see
at work on road projects, in the quarries, in
the mines, and on other tasks of hard labor are
convicted criminals, not slaves.

Prince Roald may ask your advice on court
matters, since you have not been a part of
his parents' intrigues or those of his parents'

enemies. He will be deeply grateful, I think, if the one you support first and always is him.

Forgive me for taking so personal a line, Shinko-sama, but I believe Prince Roald is lonely. I know that he is shy. It is not easy to be the child of beautiful, charming, strong-willed monarchs who took control at a very chaotic time. They have forced great changes on the realm, making enemies of some of their most powerful nobles, and have spent most of their children's lives in combat. Those children have often been in danger, and all they know sometimes is that their first duty is to the kingdom. It would be good for the prince if, in your case, the kingdom had a kind, human face.

Public meals

We shall continue our exploration of Tortallan food, table manners, and conversation on our journey east. I know these things are proving difficult for you, as you are used to the neatness of eating sticks, the difference between our food and yours, and the way our public meals are staged. Among your own household, you may dine as you please, but I hope you will make allowance for the Tortallans who will be serving you. Yamani utensils and manners will be as difficult for them as Tortallan ways are for you. In time, our ways will become more familiar.

I understand that dining with both sexes, and with a partner not your husband, will also take getting used to. (Now you know why Piers-san and I took so many meals at home, rather than dine separately at noble houses. We enjoy our mealtime talks!) Treat your partners at meals with your usual courtesy, and you will do well. I know you will be careful to converse equally with each, so that neither takes offense. Lady Cythera should be able to learn beforehand who your dinner partners will be. She will tell you something about them so you will be better able to find a subject they enjoy. It is very fortunate that you are an excellent poet, archer, hawker, and rider, as there are few noblemen in Tortall who are not interested in at least one of these subjects, if not in that of the Islands in general. If you are the highest in rank, it is expected that you will begin the conversation. If the person seated on the side closest to Their Majesties is higher to you in rank—in your case, this would be one of Their Majesties, a visiting monarch, or His Highness, your husband—that person must begin the conversation. After you have spoken with that person sufficiently, you begin conversation with the person on your other side, who sits farther from Their Majesties.

Please steel yourself with regard to table behavior. Some of our rough country noblemen disdain polished manners, feeling that they lose their manhood if they try to act as those reared in the palace do. They will wipe their mouths on their sleeves, blow their noses on the ground or on their napkins, chew with their mouths open, bellow for their glasses or cups to be filled, and belch when they have had their fill. They disdain the use of the finger bowls or splash vigorously in them. Their ladies do better—it is their instinct to copy the queen, though some pride themselves on behavior that is as "bluff" and "hearty" as that of the men. Such persons must never guess that you are repulsed by their conduct, Shinko-sama. Those who are hotheaded will cry insult should you so much as widen your eyes. The clever ones will become your enemy—and the enemy of His Highness and of your future children. Many are already the enemies of Their Majesties and only look for an opportunity to go to their allies and say, "She is our enemy, too."

The insults of commoners

When combat is not in question, should anyone below you in rank treat you with disrespect, you must allow your guards to settle the matter. Sadly, given the difference in

manners between the Islands and the Eastern
Lands, there will be occasions when you will be
insulted in public by word or gesture. (Please
note: As I told you before, unlike the Islands,
here it is not considered a combat insult to call
someone an animal name, such as monkey, cat,
dog, and so forth. Some of these are even used
affectionately. Allow your guards to judge such
insults.) There are many offensive gestures in
use in the Eastern Lands, but as with verbal
insults, it is beneath you as a princess of Tortall
to pay attention to any of them. Your male
escorts—your husband or your guards—will
punish in a fitting manner any who offer you
such remarks. You must only show those who
insult you a blank face.

Killing people

The main thing for you to remember, and the
hardest, I think, is that in the Eastern Lands it
is considered unseemly for ladies to fight. You
may do so only when you have no guards at hand
and to defend your person and the lives of your
children, your husband, and his parents. You will
bring shame upon the ruling house should you
duel. Few ladies you will encounter are trained
in combat. Of these, only Queen Thayet is equal
to you in rank, and you can hardly duel your
mother-in-law! Sir Alanna of Olau and Pirate's

Swoop is the King's Champion, but her husband is only a baron, and her sword is entirely at the service of the king, your father-in-law. While she can be quite coarse at times, her bloodline is very old, her heart is good, and it would be every bit as difficult for you to duel your father-in-law's Champion as it would for you to duel your mother-in-law. Moreover, I would not put it pas Sir Alanna to refuse a challenge from you. She would feel it wrongful, as she is in the service of the realm to which you will be, in principle, wed.

Having said these things, I am certain that sooner or later you will feel it necessary to respond to an insult to your person or to defend yourself physically when attacked. This latter is more likely, as you may find yourself in a combat group with Her Majesty. In any combat, consider matters carefully, and choose your tactics to make more friends than you do enemies. Try not to kill anyone unless ordered to do so by the queen. Be sure that your ladies understand they are under the same restrictions. At present, no one here is used to the Yamani style of sword and glaive combat.

Apologies

The people of the Eastern Lands, as I have said before, will never apologize as often or as appropriately as you are accustomed to in the

Islands. They will think less of you should you apologize as often as you are accustomed to, even if you do not truly mean it. Subtlety is not appreciated in my homeland. "Please forgive me" or "Please excuse me" is the deepest spoken apology you will receive from a noble, together with a bow. Those of the merchant class, the servants' class, and the poorer classes will bow or curtsy depending upon their sex and dress, and their apologies, while graceless, will be plentiful, the more so the lower in class the offender and the greater the offense.

Your own apologies need go no further than "I apologize" or "I am sorry" to one below you in rank, together with a slight bow or curtsy. You may offer a deeper bow or curtsy to your husband and your parents-in-law, and ask them to excuse or forgive you, but you must never kneel and press your forehead to the floor as you would to the emperor. Should you offend them grossly, they will direct you to kneel, but I cannot foresee such a day in your future, my dear.

Should anyone in your service make a mistake or offend someone in some way, I know your own innate good manners will help you to apologize gracefully without injuring your personal status in any way. Should the person who has been offended demand restitution, your staff will advise you if this is proper and what is rightful if so.

As a personal note, you may consider keeping a small jar of pickled cherries and a bowl of sugared almonds in your chambers. I have it in good faith (from my daughter the squire!) that Prince Roald is quite fond of both!

I will greet you in Amakyo Seaport in two months' time.

With my greatest hopes for your marriage and my greatest affection and respect for you, Shinkokami-sama,

I am your servant,

Ilane Evleyn, Lady of Mindelan

A Diplomat's Guide to the Realm of Tortall

In the Reign of Their Royal Majesties
King Jonathan
and Queen Thayet of Tortall

Greetings, Gentle Reader.

As you may be new to Tortall, this Guide is intended to ease your path and reduce unfortunate misunderstandings that may take place while you serve here as a member of your nation's Diplomatic Corps. Be you an Ambassador Extraordinary and Plenipotentiary, Ambassador's Aide, or a worker in the employ of your country's Embassy, you will find that reading this Guide will aid you in better understanding Tortall's laws, customs, and practices, some of which may seem unusual to you but which Tortallans hold very dear.

Introduction

Bordered by Scanra in the North, the Great Inland Sea in the South, the River Drell in the East, and the Emerald Ocean in the West, Tortall is well located for trade in the Eastern Lands. The Drell allows for easy river access with Galla, Tusaine, and Tyra, as does the Great Inland Sea with Carthak and the Southern Lands, and the Emerald Ocean with the Copper Isles and the Yamani Islands.

The Tortallan population consists of a white-skinned majority with a brown-skinned tribal minority known as the Bazhir, which is believed to have originated in the Southern Lands. Now the Bazhir live largely in the Great Southern Desert of

Tortall. While the tribes were under the theoretical control of the realm when centuries of conflict ended with King Jasson's Treaty of Persopolis in 390 H.E., few Tortallans had amicable dealings with the Bazhir until 438 H.E., when then Prince Jonathan was adopted into the Bazhir's Bloody Hawk tribe. Shortly afterward, he became a spiritual leader known as "the Voice of the Tribes," a position of great influence and advisory power, which includes a seat on their Tribal Council—the first nonnative Bazhir to be chosen. As a result of King Jonathan's unique position among the Bazhir, a significant minority have begun to integrate more fully into Tortallan society.

Slavery was formally abolished in Tortall in 249 H.E., by order of King Roger III ("Roger the Liberator"). It was the first nation in the Eastern Lands to do so. Long a haven for refugees, Tortall continued that tradition of freedom when, in 452 H.E., at the end of the Immortals War, King Jonathan permitted all Immortals who swore loyalty to the Tortallan Crown to live peacefully there, with the right to become full Subjects of the Crown with all rights pertaining thereto should they so choose.

In late 439 H.E., King Jonathan wed deposed Saren Princess Thayet jian Wilima and raised her to the position of co-monarch of Tortall. Queen Thayet not only rules alongside her husband, she also formed and rides to battle with the fighting command known as the Queen's Riders. King Jonathan also chose the first woman knight in centuries, Sir Alanna of Barony Olau and Pirate's Swoop, to be his Champion.

In addition to her other duties, in 440 H.E., Queen Thayet began an extensive school-building program throughout the realm, which continues to this day. As a result, Tortall can currently claim as high a literacy rate among its Noble and Merchant Classes as the Kingdom of Tyra, as well as a growing literacy rate among its Lower Orders.

Although all Gods and Goddesses are worshipped in Tortall as in most parts of the Eastern Lands, a majority of the men of the noble classes claim a special relationship with Mithros the Sun God. Most women of all classes claim a special relationship with the Great Mother Goddess and pray to her more than to any other deity. The Goddess is also invoked in Tortall's (and Galla's, Tusaine's, Tyra's, and Maren's) "Goddess Councils"—women's-only courts for the handling of domestic matters, as well as issues and crimes dealing with spouse and child abuse, and rape. While these seem as if they might usurp the position of the royal courts, they are dependent upon a woman or child bringing a charge before the temple court, which many are reluctant to do.

Summation

Capital: Corus

Official Language: Common, as in the language common to all the Eastern Lands (Galla, Tusaine, Tyra, Maren, and Sarain) in addition to that country's own tongue, should it have one

Population: 15 million

Rulers: At present, co-monarchs

Peoples:

- White majority—Ninety of every hundred
- Bazhir tribal Minority—Seven of every hundred
- Immortals—One of every hundred
- Other Nationals Resident in Tortall (Carthaki, Yamani, Raka)—Two of every hundred

Religions: the many gods of the Eastern Lands

Literacy:

- Among noble/knight class—Ninety-Five of every hundred
- Among merchant class—Ninety-Eight of every hundred
- Among lower classes—Forty-Five of every hundred

Size: Twenty-two to twenty-four days' ride north–south (dependent upon conditions and hostiles); fourteen and one-half days' ride east–west

Currency:

Gold noble, equal to 10 silver nobles, silver noble equal to fifty coppers

Copper nobles (commonly referred to as "coppers")

Regarding Weapons Within the Palace:

While the number of men-at-arms you may keep with you outside the palace walls is subject to your own discretion, none may accompany you into the palace building proper. They will be escorted to waiting rooms and tended, their weapons held in safekeeping until you are prepared to leave. There are no exceptions. Should you fear for your safety while in attendance at the palace, the Palace Guard may appoint a guard for you.

Swords are not permitted to guests within ten feet of the monarchs. Guests armed in any fashion, even those with eating daggers, are not allowed in the nursery or magistrate's wing. Should they be found with other, more serious and hidden weaponry, they will be held and questioned.

No weapons of any kind are acceptable within temple grounds and in holy spaces, with the exception of those held by temple guards.

All duels must be fought before witnesses, in a prepared space, with a priest of Mithros as referee, a healer, and any priests the combatants care to have present.

During a period of war, it is forbidden to issue any challenges. Those who receive them may refuse without loss of honor. During war, a noble's arms, blood, and resources belong to the Crown, not to himself.

Feast, Festival, and Holiday Dates

Awakening: First of February

    The door of the year opens. The Crone steps through, but the Spring Maiden only stirs in her sleep. Shepherds bring the pregnant ewes to the Goddess's temple for the Mother to bless them with an easy birthing and healthy young ones. As sheep go in the bitterness of winter's end, so will the other flocks in the kinder spring and summer.

Spring Equinox: Twentieth of March

    The door between winter and spring opens. The Spring Maiden steps through as the Crone withers away. Fresh reeds are placed on the altars of Mithros and the Great Mother in thanks for the return of warmth and the rebirth of the land. Female creatures heavy with young are blessed by the Mother.

Beltane: First of May

    Fertility. Herds are driven to grazing lands in fields and hills. People dance around the maypole for the good of the land and their families. When the bonfires burn low, couples join hands and jump over them for their own fertility. Couples also join in the shadows around the bonfires and beyond. February children are often called "Beltane babes."

Solstice: Twenty-third of June

The longest day. The door to summer opens. The Spring Maiden walks away, and Mithros reigns. Chiefly, a day to worship Mithros and his gifts. Once a time of sacrifice of the firstborn calf, lamb, or goat, but this practice has declined recently in Tortall. Figures of these animals are offered in their place. Mithros gives no sign that he objects.

Coronation Day: July's full moon

In celebration of the coronation of Their Royal Majesties, King Jonathan IV and Queen Thayet. (In truth, only King Jonathan was crowned on this day; Her Majesty was crowned when they wed in November of that year, in a quiet ceremony, due to famine at the time.)

Harvest: First of August

A celebration before the greatest work of the harvest is held. The first fruits of the harvest are placed on the altars of Mithros and the Goddess, and feasts are held in their name.

Fall Equinox: Twenty-third of September

The door between summer and winter opens.
Mithros steps through, and the Hunt Gods enter.
Trappers and hunters go to their temples to have
their weapons blessed. Hoofs and claws from
earlier hunts are left as offerings. Cooks offer the
first jellies to the Goddess.

All Hallow: Thirty-first of October

The first of two days dedicated to the Black
God. On All Hallow the dead who are missed
are honored with offerings of dried flowers and
sweets. Children go from house to house at sunset
collecting the offerings and carrying them to the
god's temples. They must be indoors by dark,
when the spirits of the dead may escape the god
and return to visit those who have wronged them.
This is also a time when those whose consciences
are clear may choose to wear disguises and
celebrate with singing, dancing, and feasting.

Heroes' Day: First of November

The Black God's second day, beginning at dawn,
when the escaped dead are recaptured by his
servants. At dawn, the great rulers and heroes
of the past are honored with songs, parades,
and cakes given to the poor as offerings and as
thank-yous to the children who collected sweets
on the previous day. Many have the children

identify the symbol of the monarch or hero on the cake before they may take it.

Midwinter: The week of December twenty-third

The Hunt Gods open the door and step through; the Crone of Winter enters. Gifts are exchanged and festivities held all week long in honor of the year gone by. Candles, lamps, and torches are burned throughout the fourth night, the longest night of the year, to tell Mithros he is welcome to return.

Cooper Family Papers

Timeline of the Realm of Tortall

by the hand of Thom of Pirate's Swoop, aged 10
February 22, 453 H.E.

I have to do this timeline because my tutor thinks I am an "ignorant little ape" just because I hid from him all day yesterday and read what I wanted to instead of listening to him natter.

Before Human Era (B.H.E.), the era of the Northern Empire (N.E.), the realm that held the Eastern Empire, the Southern Empire, and the Floating Empire

Who cares about the Northern Empire? It was going to pieces—that's why there was a Southern Empire, an Eastern Empire, and a Floating Empire in the west! It says in the Book of the Northern Empire that Asaron I's stupid father "loved his sons too dearly to put one over another, and so it was that Romnan of the Many Heirs divided his kingdom between them." I'm almost eleven, and I know that's folly! All the Rethawards fought with their cousins, and in the end, their nobles cried a pox on them and there was no empire at all. Only a lot of people who spoke the same language when they declared war on each other. Catch King Jonathan ever making a decision as stupid as Romnan's.

609 Asaron I of Rethaward, Emperor of the Eastern Empire, which held all of what became Tortall, Barzun, Maren, Tusaine, Tyra, and Galla

He had the calendars done up to say "A.E.," Asaron's Era, which must have been confusing for the people in the Southern Empire and the Floating Empire. Now everyone just calls it B.H.E., Before the Human Era, anyway.

Asaron spent most of his time riding around the Eastern Lands and listening to people complain about the changes in the law, the books say. I bet they complained about the new calendar, too.

644 Asaron II, "the Hopeful"

His da ruled a very long time, even with all of the riding and complaining.

653 Asaron III, "the Warrior"

He fought with his neighbors every summer and taxed his nobles to pay for it so they were too poor to give him any trouble. He also married his children to his favorites so they would protect him from any noble enemies. He wasn't stupid, for a warrior.

688 Asaron IV, "the Gracious"

Who cares if an emperor is nice to everybody?

703 Asaron V

I bet he was so mean that his people were too afraid of him to give him a nickname.

707 Strassic I, "the Unlucky"

He was a Rethaward second cousin and a baby when they killed Asaron V and crowned Strassic. When he was grown, he had three wives. They all died.

738 Strassic II, "the Great"

He was a splendid warrior. Nobody else could lift his big sword. He was killed in battle and the ladies cried and made him a shroud all of flowers.

752 Strassic III, "the Small"

If I say why I really think he was named the Small, my tutor will cane me.

At this point, Thom, I suggest that yo
write with less wit and more learning.

766 Strassic IV

This one was too boring for a nickname. He made up more laws I have to learn.

771 Strassic V, "the Fertile"

The ancients already made the jest for me. He had many children, all girls.

780 to 795 Civil war. The fall of the Eternal Dominion. Civil war. The parting of the Eastern and Southern Empires.

788 Strassic VI, "the Weak"

This is true, because he couldn't make his nobles mind him. Mayhap if he had been a strong emperor, we might still be part of the Northern Empire at least. Mama could be the Imperial Champion, and Da could travel more.

788 The Choking of the Drell

A huge earthquake destroyed the Eastern Empire's capital on the river. It raised the land and made a waterfall and a lake. Ships couldn't sail north of the middle of Tortall and Maren. Everyone believed it was because the gods turned away from the Rethaward Emperors.

795 Newlin I Conté, founder of Tortall, creates The Book of Gold, founds the College of Heralds

832 Newlin II (grandson of Newlin I)

I hope he wasn't in a hurry to inherit. I hope his da wasn't in a hurry, because he got old and died and never was king.

836 Official date of the expulsion of immortals from the Mortal Realm to the Realms of the Gods

845 Roald I of Tortall, co-regnant with Annable of Tortall

Co-rulers, like Their Majesties! Roald and Annable adopted her nephew Ennalt, renamed Newlin, when seers said no children would be born to them.

887 Newlin III, who was born Ennalt

He was old when he inherited—41.

899 Roald II, "the Virtuous"

He must have been even more boring than Strassic IV.

900 A.E. (Asaron's Era)/01 H.E. (Human Era)
The era was named by the united Schools of Heraldry in celebration of the casting out of the immortals in the former Three Empires.

- the Eastern Empire, now the Eastern Lands: Galla, Tusaine, Tortall, Maren, Barzun
- the Southern Empire, now the Carthaki Empire (formerly Carthak): Amar, Apal, Ekallatum, Shusin, Yamut, Zallara
- the Floating Empire, now the Kyprin (Copper) Isles and the Yamani Islands, and Scanra

01 Human Era in the modern calendar

Actual date of expulsion of immortals from the Mortal Realms by a great conference of mages assembled in Carthak

Uncle Numair says he isn't sure all of the immortals were banished from all of the Mortal Realms, only ones from lands that were part of the original empire. He thinks there may be immortals on the far side of the world who were never touched by the ban—they just couldn't come here. He got the idea from books he has been collecting.

01 Creation of The Book of Silver

19 Gareth I Conté, co-regnant with Doras of Great Minch

33 Gareth I Conté, co-regnant with Merice of Queenscove

57 Gareth I Conté, co-regnant with Andrette of Tameran

He was very long-lived. He had five daughters, four sons, eighteen grandchildren, and twenty-four great-grandchildren.

Baird II was his third great-grandson by Doras. I wonder how many heralds it took to keep track of his descendants?

74 Baird II, "the Lucky"

I guess because out of all those descendants, he's the one who got to be king.

75 Giamo of Galla is first seen wearing the Dominion Jewel

I wish I could see it, but Their Majesties keep it hidden.

76 to 77 Giamo of Galla conquers much of eastern Scanra

82 to 125 The Tyrant Wars

Giamo of Galla takes parts of northeast Tortall, northern Maren

Mama says it's because of all the time spent fighting the Gallans and Scanrans that our northerners are so fierce.

86 Roger I, "the Unlucky"

He tripped on his way to be crowned.

89 Roger I killed in battle with Drell River hill tribes
Jonathan II, "the Lion"

He had to fight Scanrans, Yamanis, <u>and</u> Gallans.

90 Giamo of Galla dies

(of steel poisoning by one of his own bodyguards stabbing him, Grandda says)

91 Parrac the Quiet inherits the throne of the Gallan Empire

Miache Waterborn steals the Dominion Jewel

The Gallan Empire falls apart as rivals to Parrac the Quiet fight to grab what Giamo built

The Tyran Council of Seven is founded with the aid of Miache Waterborn and Zefrem the Bear, a mercenary.

The Council of Seven offers what Grandda says was rumored to be an unheard-of bargain. The Council offered to let certain nations place money in Tyran banks. The money was guaranteed by Tyran jewels against theft, which a nation's

representative could inspect. Grandda said that not only could a country keep some money safely out of any problems that might come up at home, but their money could earn extra if it was loaned out by the Tyran bank. Within 20 years, Tyra became the keeper of funds for Carthak, Siraj, Ekallatum, Amar, Apal, Maren, Galla, and Barzun, as well as for individual nobles and merchants in those countries. Later on it will also serve Tusaine, Maren, and Tortall. The best part, Grandda says, is that no one ever attacks Tyra now because they fear that they will endanger the emergency money of entire nations, who will then come after them.

Sometime over the next ten years, the Dominion Jewel vanishes from Tyra. Miache and Zefrem, who were still advising the Council, left the government and went on a journey of several years. They returned to Tyra at last, but they lived as ordinary people. Zefrem died in 162, and Miache died two weeks after him. I want to be the Bear when I am older and find a woman like her.

101 Founding of Sarain

119 Jonathan II, "the Lion of Tortall," is assassinated

Grandda says his people got tired of all of the fighting. Da says more like they tired of paying taxes for it. Someone put so much dreamrose in the Lion's supper wine that he died.

119 Baird III, "the Adamant"

He forgot to find out who poisoned his father. Da says that's a matter of knowing when not to wake a snoring lion.

To my lord baron and his honorable father-in-law, I would be grateful if you would refrain from adding to my instruction to the children with regard to history. To learn so many conflicting, cynical views of the fa confuses the children and makes it harder for them.

125 Treaty of the Falls

The end of the last Gallan war. The treaty was signed by the kings of Maren, Tortall, and Galla on a big field full of flowers beside the lake in the Drell. There were priests and priestesses from the City of the Gods to bless it. The City was being built then.

Baird III dies

Regency of Roger II

He was five. A council of lords ruled until he came of age.

174 Landless white nobles attack the Copper Isles

177 Roger II ends his regency

He is called the Wall Builder in all of the books, but most of the walls he built have since fallen down. He should have watched the builders.

181 Jasson I, co-regnant with Sidea of Naxen

Here's another one! A man trading in our village said there's never been a king and a queen governing at the same time, but in my books, it happens often in the Eastern Lands, except for Sarain! Gareth I had <u>three</u> queens co-regnant!

Queen Dilsubai of the Copper Isles is betrayed to white invaders and slain. Oronden Rittevon, the first Rittevon king, is crowned ruler of the Copper Isles. Isn't this stealing? Why didn't any of the rulers of the Eastern Lands do something?

200 Gareth II, "the Stern"

(He was born Henrim and adopted by Jasson I from his Queenscove cousin's family, since Jasson never married and had no heirs otherwise. He changed his name to be a proper Conté.)

204 <u>The Book of Copper</u>

208 Norren III of Maren seen wearing Dominion Jewel

210 Noren III marries Anj'la from Manai in Apal, the Southern Lands

He crowns her co-regnant with him.
(Apal is in what is now Carthak.)

222 Prince Roger of Tortall marries Alyzy of Galla

224 Roger III, "the Liberator," marries Jessamine of Barzun

246 Birth of Prince Gareth

251 to 280 The Era of the Civil Wars in Tortall

They were also called the Slave Wars. A great many of the rebels didn't want to free their slaves despite the king's vow after his son was kidnapped and made to serve as a slave. The rebels didn't want to pay former slaves for labor. Grandda says this is when House haMinch rose to power because of their loyalty to the crown, along with Legann, Naxen, and Queenscove. My parents are great friends with the present lords of Legann, Queenscove, and Naxen, and some of the people of haMinch, but not all of them, because many of their lords think it is wrong for Mama to be a knight.

278 Gareth III, "the Builder"

He repaired city walls and fortresses all during his reign and lent his nobles money at a good rate of interest so they could repair theirs. He also arranged for many former slaves to work on his building projects so they could learn trades. He ended the Civil Wars with executions of the heads of noble houses who were still in rebellion. Then he brought the families of the new heads of the noble houses to live at court during half of the year, and sent them to live at home during the other half, when their lord came to live at court. This practice was continued until 323. He did this so that some part of each noble family would be in his control all of the time. Mama says this is very wrong, but Da says it's just the way he would have done it in the king's shoes.

280 The Era of the Civil Wars ends

299 to 308 The Nine Years' Famine in Maren

Actually this was a time of many wars and famines because armies fought on the fields and killed the crops, or when they weren't fighting on them, they were marching across them. The Marenite king Qual the Foolish got into a border war with Sarain and a sea war with Siraj (now part of Carthak). To pay for it, he ordered the treasury to give out coins that were short weight in metal, so he could use the extra metal to make more coins. The merchants and bankers found out and raised their prices. The nobles found out just as the king raised taxes on the nobles he didn't like, and they waged war against him and each other. It all sounds very stupid and messy.

304 Founding of Tusaine

The nobles of eastern Maren broke off from their country to make their own realm and stole part of the land on our side of the Drell as well. We have been fighting over that land ever since. Mama was in the last war.

308 Kirikene the Clever of Maren

Sarain and Siraj signed peace treaties with Maren. King Qual shaved his head and took vows of silence as a priest of the Black God and became a preparer of the dead. His nobles chose his cousin Kirikene the Clever to be queen. They thought a woman would be easier to control, but she turned out to be a very strong and wise queen. Grandda said her nobles never knew what she might do next. Her consort loved her and would not allow anyone to try to make him rule in her place. She made peace throughout the realm, fixed the coins, and said to let Tusaine go, as they were all troublemakers anyway.

321 Wylles the Sickly

That was the end of that name for kings! (Wylles, not Sickly.)

Less levity, more information, Thom.

323 Jasson II (regency of Queen Margarry)

The queen ordered the end of the custom of keeping the nobles at court for half the year. She said it was too expensive.

326 The last person to have been a slave in Tortall dies

339 Jasson II, "Goddess-Blessed," his majority, end of regency

He built a convent and suggested that his mother the regent take vows and become the Head Daughter of it.

346 Roald III, "the Horse-Tamer"

My mother's horse Darkmoon was sired by His Majesty's Darkness, who comes from one of the Horse-Tamer's lines of mounts.

348 Rebellion of the scythes

This rebellion was against taxes on crops brought to market. Farmers burned grain in the fields rather than harvest for tax collectors. The Horse-Tamer was fatally wounded as he put down one of the many revolts.

351 Roger IV, "the Ill-Fated"

He died of a cold contracted when he was bear hunting in the mountains. He didn't take a mage with him, and he refused to turn back for "a ridiculous fit of the sneezes."

353 Roald IV, "the Quiet" (adopted House Legann nephew of Roger IV)

He wrote a law that requires all members of the royal family to be accompanied by a mage who is an acknowledged master of healing whenever they are not in any of the royal residences.

367 Baird IV, "the Roisterer"

368 Prince Jasson born

386 Prince Jasson marries Daneline of Jesslaw in Barzun

393 Prince Roald born

395 Prince Jasson retakes the western bank of the River Drell from Tusaine

396 Jasson III, "the Fierce," the General

400 Barzun conquered by Jasson III

415 Battle of Joyous Forest on the borders with
     Tusaine and Galla

417 Prince Roald marries Liane of Naxen

422 Jasson III abdicates in favor of his son Roald

422 Roald V, "the Peacemaker"

439 Jonathan IV

440 Marriage to Thayet, co-regnant
     Roald (born 440)
     Kalasin (born 441)
     Liam (born 442)
     Jasson (born 443)
     Lianne (born 445)
     Vania (born 446)

443 Thom of Pirate's Swoop born (me!)

445 Alan and Alianne of Pirate's Swoop born (twin pains)

> Ideally, you and your siblings
> do not belong here, Thom, on
> a list of royalty.

November 12, 456

Thom—

I dug out my notes on the Mages
College—and added in some new ones,
from what I remember—and put them into
some sort of order, a rough outline of
what would be expected over four years
for both general magecraft and for healing
students. Your mother didn't mention
where your interests lie, so you can pore
over or ignore my various scribblings as
you find them useful.

My best to the Baron and to Alan and
Alianne,

Neal

To the student healers, from Duke Baird
of Queenscove, Chief Healer of the Realm,
greetings and most welcome.

In all places, throughout history, those
with a healing Gift have learned to use it
at the side of another, grinding herbs in a
stillroom and following the older healer from
house to house to visit patients.* With the idea
that the traditional model was sound, I met
with Their Majesties and Master Harailt in
August of 441 H.E. to discuss a program
for healers at the newly conceived Tortallan
Mages College. Though our scope is expanded
from the old apprenticeships, and owes much
to the Carthaki University, at its heart there
remains a deep regard for the connection that
healers form with other healers: their mentors,
their friends, their students. We are a strong
community with a strong commitment to ease
our fellow man and honor the gods who Gifted
us. The work is not easy, but no matter how
far it takes us—into battlefields and plague
tents, toward floods, fires, and earthquakes—
we do it together. Gods all bless.

Baird of Queenscove

*He got this bit from Mother,
or I'll eat my favorite boots.—Neal

Healers' Course of Study

History and Ethics
Geoffrey Calvard

Everyone in the Mages College takes this. The subject is fascinating, but Calvard is a cantankerous old fusspot. Really, if you must seek out first-year students to inform them that you're a tough instructor no matter whose father is the Chief Healer, you need a nap and a strong ~~calming draught~~ laxative. His book on mages in the Slave Wars is very good, though.

Non-healing students also study Old Thak, astronomy, and basic elemental magics in the first year. Some of the instructors cross over—Eliora of Fenrigh works in the Royal Hospital and teaches fire magic, the pair who teach herbs also teach forest and earth magic, and you'll see my father at Mages talking about the role of magic in community health, or Numair Salmalín will come over to Healers and tell us about battle magic from his side of it. There are a lot of short lecture series like that, built around very busy or visiting mages' schedules. Even the king teaches sometimes!

Healer's Practical
Blayce of Carmine Tower and
Eleni of Olau

Students meet in small, informal groups to learn
and practice basic healing magics, non-magical
care, and meditation. Blayce is a good sort,
young, talks very fast, and I am positively green
with envy that Mother Cooper is truly your
grandmother—do you think she would adopt me?
There is a similar class for other mage students,
lots of meditation and learning to control
whatever magics you discovered as a child.

Anatomy
Evaline of Tasride

Cornerstone of the healer's program, obviously.
There are books and charts and wax models and,
so to speak, examples, but I recommend learning
to draw or making friends with a good artist.
Don't eat right before class.

Herbal Cures
Odeen Estvell, Aniki Nissyen

Learning to identify herbs, dry and store them,
make all types of preparations, how and when to

magically enhance them. We go tromping around the Royal Forest without warning, so wear boots and bring a hat if it looks like rain.

In the second and third years, students begin working in the Royal Hospital, assisting with supplies, linens, bathing and feeding patients, and changing bandages. How different my life has become! I would rhapsodize further on the glories of knighthood, but I have some bandages to change. . . .

Disease and Remedy
Nerina Greyson

More or less retraces the anatomy class, only this time you learn what can go wrong and how to heal it. Starts with healing the sniffles and works up to knife, axe, and sword wounds.

Third-year students may add a class in the Natural Sciences, Literature and Rhetoric, Mathematics, or Engineering. Private instruction in music and the noble arts is available outside the course of study, but there was no availing on my part—as Father likes to remind me, not even he can heal tone deafness. Duties at the Royal Hospital increase for healers, and the other mage students begin working for and with a single mentor, someone at the University or based at the palace who shares your interests.

As I am duty-bound to obey the Lady Alanna, and especially as she is reading over my shoulder at the moment telling me what to write, I will add that you don't have to choose between healing and other magics. Harailt of Aili will help you find whatever training you need and fit it together: Marketa of Lisafer is studying healing and weather magic, and my friend Asma bin Haytham divided her studies between Corus and the Bazhir school.

To Neal—

Thank you for the notes. They are helping me picture what University will be like. It sounds very busy and interesting, but not too exciting, which I think is good. Did you send these poems by accident? I thought you might want them back to keep with the rest of your poetry. I hope it gets to you safely and finds you and Ma in good health.

—Thom

P.S. Is "The Skeleton" about Evaline of Tasride? I think so because she is the anatomy teacher. My da agrees. He says I needn't say so in my letter, only I want to know if I guessed it. Please write back soon!

The Skeleton
4th September, 451

Bones are living tissue, of three layers: dense
bone, soft bone, and marrow. They are not dead
or inert! If they were, we couldn't heal them!
She speaks with marvelous passion.

Every word has beauty from her lips

cured
heard
demurred   2 kinds of bone marrow

Imparting beauty to her every word,
She names the bones, her voice runs down my
    spine
And teaches, in the sweetest voice I've heard,
A double lesson: to name the bones, and pine

Anatomizing beauty ~~is more hard is my task~~
    is utterly hopeless!

Anatomizing beauty gives no cure
Since that my sickness in her body lies
To make her better makes my sickness more
To ease my heart, I must needs lose mine
    eyes,

243

Stop up mine nose and ears and senses all
And memory, and thought. In short, to die
Will cure this love and end my aching thrall
(Still she'll name bones while still my poor
    bones lie)
But to die for her would be to wrong her so,
That I who love her live to live in woe.

—N.

12 pairs of ribs

24 vertebrae that bend about
5 fused for hip bones to attach
then 4 more fused ("tailbone")
33 in all

Upon Watching a Yamani Lady
Playing Toss-the-Fan

Behold the war fan
Crimson-winged in the fresh breeze
Dipping among the fire lilies.

Meadow lilies? Irises? What is the most
tall, slender, and dignified? I do not know
enough about decorative plants. Is it rude to
compare ladies to flowers? Must read more
Sasukia Hama.

The shukusen speaks plainly:
You amuse me, sir.
Please stay. Please go.
Bleed.

A near thing. So many angry women in
my life. And one fiery Yamani flower who
inhabits my dreams, waking and sleeping.
Would my parents welcome a Yamani
daughter-in-law?
Would her family
welcome a gaijin
son-in-law, if
I even had the
courage to ask
her?

    —N.

Lessons with the Lioness

<u>Symbolic aid</u>

For example, bleeding: you're not actually tying the blood vessels into a knot, but you're trying to get them to STOP and a knot means STOP or BIND. Like all magical aids, thread serves as a physical expression of your will—and the more focused your will, the more effective your spell—so if I ever call it hedge magic or child's play again, the Lioness will tie me into a half hitch and leave me up a tree, and I can write that down, too, as long as I'm taking so many all-fired notes. Good gods, she says "Nealan" in exactly the same threatening tone as my mother!

If I ever learn Father's way of twisting and doubling a thread to reseal a collapsed lung onto the chest wall, try to teach it to her. Twenty-odd years and she hasn't got the trick. I think it will be years before I even try!

<u>Concentration aid</u>

More advanced or delicate work, where you're keeping track of several things at once. You could have one thread in which you invest your will to reroute blood around a damaged vessel so the arm or leg still has blood flowing, while you use another thread to heal the damage, and so forth, keeping your intentions separate and strong.

After practicing, cannot tie knots one-handed. Seems like something the Stump should have taught us, along with fishing with only our teeth and jousting with both feet tied behind our backs. But I wax nostalgic. . . .

Is there rope magic? Good question. How about fishing nets? Good question. What about thread made into a net? Isn't there something about this in—I can't recall the title—Nerina Greyson's masterwork? I long for the University library. My mistress points out, quite rightly, that instead of a library we have a lot of thread and very little to do until the rain lets up.

What about ladies with long hair? Thread magic and essence spells combined? Good question. I am beginning to suspect that "good question" means "answer it yourself, O squire."

After several hours of mending clothing and tack, I have ideas about difficult-to-stitch areas, scalp especially. My two lives, merging, as Orneyn the Wolf writes: "With every action we make our fate, a thousand thousand rivulets of melted snow, and where all tributaries meet all things are known."

Knight-mistress only said "hmm" to the

quote and poked our small fire, but today
I used a bit of thread magic to erase our
tracks, and she clapped me on the back and
said, "Does not the sea begin as every little
snowflake?" I suppose my face did something,
because she grinned and added, "Yes, I read."
Perhaps my squiredom will not be all threats
and foul weather?

April 3, 455

Letter intercepted by Sparrow Fetlock,
direct to Nursemaid Sweetening

Direct by special pouch to the Whisper Man

Sir,

Fetlock and I thought you would want to
see this right away. It came this afternoon
by way of the regular mail on the Coast
Road, not in your own pouch. From the
way it was written we thought you might
not know the contents.

Sweetening

April 2, 455

To Lord Imrah of Legann
From Alan of Pirate's Swoop

My Lord.

My mother is Sir Alanna of Pirate's Swoop and Olau. My father is the baron of Pirate's Swoop. I am ten years old.

I am old enough to train as a page. I do not wish to do so at the palace. I have heard many people say that the training master hates my mother. They say that he has said openly that she is no true knight, even though she serves the king as his Champion. I do not wish to learn about chivalry from this man.

In our history lessons our tutor told my brother and me that before Gareth III made noble families spend half the year at court and began to train pages and squires there, a boy who wished to become a knight would be the page and squire of an older knight who would teach him how to do things. My tutor says there is no law against this, only that most people prefer to send their sons to the court school.

My mother says you are a good and brave man. My father says you are wise.

Please, my lord, would you train me to be a

knight? I will do whatever you tell me, even if I have to eat bitter greens or muck out pigsties. I am very tidy and I have my own pony and saddle gear. I hunt with our family's huntsman, who has seen me bag rabbits and pheasants. I can also fish.

I wait for the honor of your reply.

Alan of Pirate's Swoop

April 4, 455

The Whisper Man to Nursemaid Sweetening

Let this go on to Lord Imrah at Port Legann without further interference.

April 10, 455

From Imrah, Lord of Port Legann

To George, Baron of Pirate's Swoop

George,

Your son has written to ask me to train him as page and squire. Were you aware of this? Is your lady wife aware of this? Under the circumstances, and given the current training master, I am inclined to take the boy on. He has always seemed like a likely lad on my visits to you, and I could use someone lively around here.

Imrah

April 10, 455

From Imrah, Lord of Port Legann
To Alan of Pirate's Swoop

Alan,
Your letter has given me much cause
for thought. You are aware that few
nobles choose this manner of training.
Usually they are those whose fiefdoms
are not wealthy enough to supply them
at court without causing their families
hardship. Do not think this will be a
way for you to avoid rude comments from
people at court, that is what I am trying
to tell you. I think the fact that I will
be responsible for your education will
protect you from all but the most ignorant
remarks (which is one of the reasons, I
must suppose, that you chose me as a
possible knight-master), but it will not
do so from those determined to insult you
and your family. That is the nature of the
world.
Before I agree to your proposal, you
must speak to both of your parents and
get their permission, in writing, for this
arrangement. They are good friends of
mine. I do not wish to put my friendship

with them at risk. Since you did not mention them in your letter, I must assume that you did not discuss your plan with them.

Should I receive letters from them indicating to me that they approve of your plan, I will write to you so that we may settle upon when you should come to me and what belongings you should bring.

Mithros guide you,

Imrah

April 15, 455

To Imrah, Lord of Port Legann

From George, Baron of Pirate's Swoop

My lord,

Thank you for your kindness to our lad. It has been hard for him, with a twin sister and an older brother who clearly show definite talents in areas requiring a great deal of cleverness. This is not to say the boy is stupid, for he is not that in the least. But he is shy and he refuses to look foolish—in his own eyes—by seeming to vie with Thom and Alianne. I have been thinking he needs a larger setting to live in, where he may work out who he is among a variety of people. Under your watchful eye, I am certain he will do well.

If ever you or your lady wife require a service of me or mine, never hold back from asking.

George

April 15, 455

To Imrah, Lord of Port Legann
From Alanna, Knight of Pirate's Swoop and Olau

My dear Imrah,

I know you will laugh when I admit I was a bit vexed to hear that my son Alan had applied to you to teach him the duties of page and squire. I had not even considered that if he chose our path, he would find another way than the conventional one. Since he has, I would have hoped that he might come to me, but after George explained things for an evening, I understand that you are a far better choice. I am still far too controversial, and it was always considered a bad idea for a father to train up his own sons to be knights. I fear I might be too harsh to my boy. That would never do. It's bad enough he has to put up with his grumpy old mother on the rare occasions when she is home.

Also, my friend, I am delighted that, however the thing was managed, you have agreed. I can't think of a better person to have the schooling of Alan, now that poor health has

forced Duke Gareth the Elder away from more
strenuous activities. I remember the few times
I've seen you fight in the Tusaine War and in
tournament jousts, and I know you are a scholar
in your own right. Thank you so much for taking
Alan on!

I know you shall be seeing more of me in the
years to come, for some reason.

I am in your debt,

Alanna

Notices from Across the Realm

Eager to serve Crown and country?
Looking for adventure and a good wage?
Join the Queen's Riders!

Roam the land, root out those who prey on
the helpless, and bring peace to those who
work to feed the kingdom. If that is the drink
to fill your cup; if you are older than 16,
healthy, and able to read, write, and do sums,

Seek your local Riders Group

Lad or lass, it makes no difference.
Skin color, realm of birth, mageborn or no,
it makes no matter.

Join for the adventure of a lifetime
with the Queen's Riders!

Rise Up,
Trueborn Sons & Daughters of Tortall
Our Beloved Realm Is in Danger!

Do You See the Flood of Foreign-Born Who Have Risen
to Power in the Last 20 Years?

Our King Is Wrapt in Bazhir Magic, Wed to
a Foreign Queen, Counseled by Mages from
Galla and Dread Carthak,
His Queen Guided by Foreign Savages

The Heir to Our Crown Wed to a Yamani Princess

The Knight Commander of the King's Own
Wed to a Foreigner

These outlanders fill the ranks of our knights with
women to weaken our armies!

They have opened the gates
to immortal monsters!

Who will stand against the foreigners?
Who will save our beloved realm of Tortall?

November 16, 459 H.E.

Chancellor and Whisper Man! This was just
handed to me by Vania, who had it thrust on
her as she was leaving services at the Goddess's
temple. My own child, under the very noses of
her guards! I want an explanation, I want whys
and wherefores, and I want the writers and their
fellow conspirators in person! I want bodies in
prison, on the rack, for every tear my child just
shed on my shoulder, is it understood?

Jonathan, King Co-Regnant of Cortall

In my own hand and under my own seal
By fast courier

November 16, 459

Sire,

At this moment, the Whisper Man is traveling, reports of similar flyers having reached us both. They have appeared in places as far apart as Rosetown and Hoffbrook. They have even been found in Persopolis and Port Caynn, normally strongholds for Your Majesties. A man was seen nailing one to a crier's post in Port Caynn, but sadly, he was stoned to death by onlookers before he could be captured, and thrown into the bay before a death mage could inspect the corpse. Word has been sent to the Provost's people to capture such persons alive if at all possible.

Our people are on alert, and the Whisper Man is on the hunt with our top Hostlers. Please tell your family they have nothing to fear.

The Chancellor
By my own hand
Personal courier

From Their Royal Majesties Co-Regnant,
King Jonathan and Queen Thayet of Tortall

To His Royal Majesty
King Matrurin Crozat of Galla

On this blessed day of the Gods,
December 8th
in the year 459 of the Human Era

To Our Honored Cousin, greetings!

It has come to Our attention that officers of your realm have recently entered Ours without paying Us a visit at our palace of Corus. We are filled with regret. Surely your officers did not feel uncertain of the welcome they might receive at Our hands, despite certain untruthful papers that have circulated in the marketplaces? Such has been the great friendship between Our kingdoms that it seems almost unbelievable that anyone who answers to your throne might feel it needless to call upon Us and to pursue travels about Our kingdom without notification of Our royal governors.

With regard to another matter, it has come to Our attention that Gallan royal bankers have applied to bankers of Our realm with regard to several loans in gold to be paid out as soon as possible, and for ten additional loans, already made by our bankers to yours, to be postponed for a year with regard to payment. It is with greatest regret that We have told all of the kingdom's bankers that We are unable to approve loans of any kind to Galla for the foreseeable future, with matters so uncertain between us. Indeed, We are forced to request, on Our banks' behalf, repayment of all loans to Galla that are presently outstanding. Until these affairs of finance are settled, and certain scurrilous announcements to Our populace cease, We shall have to retain all Gallan assets within our borders, keeping them safe from those uncertainties with which We are concerned.

Once these unsecure times are over, dearest cousin, We will be overjoyed to restore Our happy, peaceable relations with you and your officials once more.

May the Great and Lesser Gods smile upon you, your queen, and your children,

Jonathan, King Co-Regnant
Thayet, Queen Co-Regnant

An Official Chronology of Tortallan Events

An Official Chronology of Tortallan Events

795 Eastern Empire, Before Human Era (B.H.E.)
- Tortall founded.
- *The Book of Gold* is created.

1 Human Era (H.E.) ─────────
- *The Book of Silver* is created.

174 H.E. ─────────
- Prior to this date, Queen Imiary VI is overthrown after a twelve-year reign of the Copper Isles, by Queen Dilsubai, the last native Kyprish ruler.
- April—Rittevon of Lenman (a Marenite) begins his conquest of the Copper Isles.

181 ─────────
- June—Rittevon is crowned ruler of the Copper Isles, after the final battle on the Plain of Sorrows (where one-third of the Kyprish warriors are female).

187 ─────────
- The Crown has the breakwater built in Port Caynn.

200 ─────────
- Kyprioth's Prophecy (concerning the raka and the Copper Isles) is recorded.

204 ─────────
- *The Book of Copper* is created.

249 ─────────
- King Roger III frees all slaves in Tortall.

312 ─────────
- *The Luarin Conquest: New Rulers in the Copper Isles,* by Michabur Durse of Queenscove, is published.

378 ─────────
- The nation of Barzun is conquered by Tortall during the reign of King Jasson III.

401 ───────────────────────
- Roger of Conté is born.

405 ───────────────────────
- Liam Ironarm is born.

409 ───────────────────────
- The Battle of Joyous Forest: Coram Smythesson saves Gareth of Naxen.

413 ───────────────────────
- George Cooper is born.

415 ───────────────────────
- Ralon of Malven is born.
- Gareth (the Younger) of Naxen is born.
- Raoul of Goldenlake is born.
- Alexander of Tirragen is born.
- Francis of Nond is born.

416 ───────────────────────
- August—Prince Jonathan of Conté is born.

418 ───────────────────────
- Maude Laewulf's husband, Gavin, is killed while fighting bandits.

419 ───────────────────────
- May—Thom and Alanna of Trebond are born.
- Thayet *jian* Wilima is born.

424 ───────────────────────
- Arram Draper (later Numair Salmalín) is born.
- Buriram Tourakom is born.

430 ───────────────────────
Late Winter/Early Spring:
- January-ish—George Cooper becomes the King of the Rogues.
- Thom and Alanna switch places and head to the City of the Gods and the Palace (respectively) for training (March, at the latest).
    - Ralon picks on Alanna.
    - Douglass of Veldine is already a page in the palace.
    - Gary agrees to sponsor "Alan."

- May—Alanna and Thom turn eleven.
- Alanna and Gary meet George in the city.

Summer/Autumn/Winter:

- Ralon breaks Alanna's arm.
- Mid-October—Alanna's arm is completely healed.
- December—Alanna defeats Ralon shortly before Midwinter.
- Midwinter—Gary, Raoul, Alex, and other fourteen-year-olds are made squires.

431 ──────────────────

Winter/Spring:

- March—The Sweating Sickness reaches Tortall.
- Francis of Nond dies.
- Alanna saves Jon's life; Myles guesses Alanna's secret.
- Trip to Port Caynn (sometime in the spring)—Alanna begins binding her chest.
- May—Alanna and Thom turn twelve.

Summer/Autumn/Winter:

- August—Roger arrives.
- Autumn—Alanna introduces Jon to George, and they purchase Moonlight and Darkness.
- The four youngest pages (Alanna, Geoffrey, Sacherell, Douglass) begin their fencing lessons.

432 ──────────────────

Winter/Spring:

- Alanna and Sacherell duel; Sacherell trounces her.
- May 5—
  - Alanna's true identity is revealed to George.
  - She meets Eleni Cooper for the first time.
- May—Alanna and Thom turn thirteen.

Summer/Autumn/Winter:

- Trip to Barony Olau with Sir Myles; Alanna obtains Lightning.
- Winter—Jon befriends City Folk; Alex becomes Roger's squire.

Spring:
- Gary, Raoul, and Alex have reached their eighteenth birthdays; Jon will turn seventeen within the year.
- April—
  - Lord Martin arrives from Persopolis.
  - Alanna duels with Geoffrey and wins.
- Trip to Fief Meron and the Black City
  - The squires (and Alanna) meet Ali Mukhtab.
  - Jon and Alanna defeat the Ysandir.
  - Jon learns that Alanna is a girl.
- May—Alanna and Thom turn fourteen.

Summer/Autumn/Winter:
- Pages take a trip to Fief Naxen.
- Midwinter—
  - Raoul of Goldenlake passes his Ordeal of knighthood.
  - Gareth (the Younger) of Naxen passes his Ordeal of knighthood.
  - Alexander of Tirragen passes his Ordeal of knighthood.
  - Prince Jonathan of Conté passes his Ordeal of knighthood.
- Alanna becomes Jon's squire.
- Geoffrey, Sacherell, and Douglass are made Alex's, Gary's, and Raoul's squires.

Late Winter/Spring:
- Lord Alan dies.
  - Thom becomes Lord of Trebond.
  - Coram returns to Trebond.
- Alanna meets the Goddess and finds Faithful.
- May—Alanna and Thom turn fifteen.

Summer/Autumn:
- July—
  - Tusaine embassy arrives.
  - Alanna duels with Dain of Melor.

- Roger begins doubting "Alan" and sends people to keep an eye on Thom.
- August—
  - Alanna has her first kiss.
  - Jon turns nineteen.
  - Delia of Eldorne is introduced to the court.
- At some point, Adigun *jin* Wilima becomes the leader of Sarain.

435 ──────────────────────────

Winter/Spring:
- January—The squires have to camp out in the Royal Forest; a boar attacks Alanna.
- Gary and Raoul fight a duel over one of Delia's riding gloves; they are sent on border patrol.
- March—Alex and Alanna duel.
- April—George gives Alanna information about Tusaine that she passes on to Myles.
- King Roald sends out a Call to Muster.
- Alanna and company fight in the war against Tusaine.
  - Roger confronts Alanna.
  - Alanna gets captured.
  - Jon defies the king to lead a rescue mission.
- May—Alanna and Thom turn sixteen.

Summer/Autumn:
- August—A peace treaty with Tusaine is signed; the army returns to Corus.
- Alanna appeals to Eleni Cooper to teach her about a woman's life.

Winter:
- The palace hunts for a wolf named Demon Grey.

436 ──────────────────────────

Spring:
- Late January—Veralidaine Sarrasri is born in Galla.
- May—
  - Alanna and Thom turn seventeen.
  - Alanna and Jon become lovers.

Autumn/Winter:
- October—Queen Lianne falls ill.
- Uline of Hannalof is born.

Spring:
- Around this time, Dusan *zhir* Anduo tries to overthrow Adigun *jin* Wilima for the Saren throne.
- April—
  - George and Alanna travel to the City of the Gods, where Thom has become a Master.
  - George is nearly killed on the way home.
- May—Alanna and Thom turn eighteen.

Summer/Autumn/Winter:
- Alanna confesses her identity to Gary.
- October-ish—Civil war begins in Sarain.
- December—
  - Midwinter: Alanna passes her Ordeal of knighthood.
  - Second Feast of Midwinter:
    - Alanna duels with Duke Roger.
    - Alanna's identity is revealed to the court.
- Douglass of Veldine, Geoffrey of Meron, and Sacherell of Wellam pass their Ordeals of knighthood.

Winter/Spring/Summer:
- New Year's Day—Alanna and Coram head south.
- Alanna finds a crystal sword.
- Alanna and Coram join the Bloody Hawk Bazhir tribe.
- Ali Mukhtab arrives at the Bloody Hawk camp.
  - Mukhtab reveals himself to Alanna as the Voice of the Tribes.
  - He brings a written history of the Bazhir for Jonathan.
- Coram rides north to fetch Jonathan.
- Akhnan Ibn Nazzir tries to kill Alanna with the crystal sword.
  - Alanna kills him and takes possession of the sword.
  - She (unwillingly) becomes the tribe's shaman.

- Alanna begins training apprentices.
- Shaman-apprentices have their first battle.
- A week later, the "shaman school" begins when other shamans visit the Bloody Hawk.
- Myles and Jon arrive.
- Jon passes his trial by combat and becomes a Bazhir.
- Alanna has her adoption ceremony with Myles; Kara and Kourrem are witnesses—a first for Bazhir women.
- The full moon—Kara and Kourrem pass the Rite of Shamans.
- Fifteen days later (at the new moon)—
  - Jon becomes the Voice of the Tribes.
  - Ali Mukhtab dies.
- Alanna and Coram travel to Port Caynn to visit George.
  - Coram meets Rispah.
- Kalasin, wife to Warlord Adigun *jin* Wilima in Sarain, commits suicide.
- May—Alanna and Thom turn nineteen.
- August or September—Nealan of Queenscove is born.

439

Winter/Spring/Summer:
- King Roald introduces Page Examinations.
- January—Alanna and Coram travel south, one week after George leaves.
- Halef Seif sends Alanna to Lake Tirragen to help the sorceress of Alois.
- Days later, before dying, the sorceress gives Alanna the map to the Dominion Jewel and the spell to fix Lightning by merging it with the crystal sword.
- March—Alanna and Coram show up in Berat to find Nahom Jendrai.
  - Alanna meets Liam Ironarm.
  - Queen Lianne dies.
  - King Roald dies in a hunting "accident" three weeks later.

- April—Alanna, Coram, and Liam head out of Maren.
  - Liam begins teaching Shang fighting to Alanna.
- Alanna meets Thayet *jian* Wilima and Buriram Tourakom (plus the children traveling with them) and escorts them to Rachia.
- April/May—The Great Market Riot takes place in Corus.
- May—
  - Alanna's traveling company passes Sarain's eastern border and heads to the Roof of the World.
  - A Doi seer tells the party their futures.
  - The Dominion Jewel is secured for Tortall.
  - Alanna and Thom turn twenty.
- Raoul meets up with Alanna, and they all travel back to Tortall.
- Alanna is made the King's Champion, sixty days before the coronation (and two days after her return to Tortall).
- June—Beltane
  - Jon pardons George and ennobles him.
  - Alanna has her last meeting with the Goddess and meets the pantheon of deities of the Eastern Lands.
  - June/July—Master Si-cham comes to Corus to deal with the side effects of Roger's resurrection.
- July—the day of the full moon
  - Jonathan is crowned king of Tortall.
  - Master Si-cham is murdered.
  - Duke Gareth of Naxen suffers a heart attack.

Autumn:
- Famine in Tortall as a result of the use of the Dominion Jewel.
- October (second week)—
  - Buri and Thayet visit Alanna.
  - Alanna gives Thayet and Jonathan her blessing.
  - The Wildcat (Eda Bell) brings Liam's letter to Alanna.
- King Jonathan announces his engagement to Princess Thayet.
- George proposes; Alanna accepts.

440 ———————————————

- Education becomes available to all Tortallans; schools are opened throughout the realm.
- Prince Roald of Conté is born.
- Maura of Dunlath is born.
- Joren of Stone Mountain is born.
- Cleon of Kennan is born.
- Vinson of Genlith is born.
- Balduin of Disart is born.
- Zahir ibn Alhaz is born.
- Garvey of Runnerspring is born.

441 ———————————————

- Princess Kalasin of Conté is born.
- Faleron of King's Reach is born.
- Yukimi noh Daiomoru is born.

442 ———————————————

- King Jonathan and Queen Thayet proclaim that girls can train for knighthood.
- Ozorne is crowned Emperor of Carthak.
- Thayet establishes the Queen's Riders.
- June—Keladry of Mindelan is born.
- Merric of Hollyrose is born.
- Seaver of Tasride is born.
- Quinden of Marti's Hill is born.
- Lord Wyldon of Cavall takes the position of page training master.

443 ———————————————

- Prince Liam of Conté is born.
- Thom of Pirate's Swoop is born.
- Owen of Jesslaw is born.
- Prosper of Tamaran is born.
- Teron of Blythdin is born.
- Arram Draper flees Carthak and changes name to Numair Salmalín.

444 ———————————————

- Prince Jasson of Conté is born.

- Warric of Mandash is born.
- Iden of Vikison Lake is born.

445 ——————————————

- Princess Lianne of Conté is born.
- Alan and Alianne of Pirate's Swoop are born.

446 ——————————————

- Princess Vania of Conté is born.
- Sairayu Balitang is born.
- Baron Piers of Mindelan and his family go to the Yamani Islands, representing the Crown.
- Timon Greendale reorganizes the palace service.

447 ——————————————

- Carthaki mages find the spells to open the Divine Realms (during the eighth year of King Jonathan's reign).
- Ilane of Mindelan saves Yamani relics (swords) from invading pirates.
- Salma Aynnar joins the palace staff (while Conal of Mindelan is still training).
- Sir Raoul is thrown from the saddle in a jousting match; he is defeated.

448 ——————————————

- Kel of Mindelan begins training on glaive.

449 ——————————————

Winter:
- Daine's family is attacked; she loses her home.

Spring:
- March—Onua Chamtong hires Daine at the Cría fair.
- Daine is visited by the Badger God for the first time.
- Daine meets Numair.
- Lord Sinthya escapes to Carthak.
- April—
   ○ Daine and company arrive in Corus.
   ○ Daine takes a job with the Riders and learns about wild magic.
   ○ Stormwings attack the palace.

- May—
  - King Jonathan rides on Progress.
  - Queen Thayet and her Riders move out for Pirate's Swoop.
  - Daine begins to learn how to heal animals.
  - Riders encounter griffins on the coast.
- Pirate's Swoop is surrounded by an unmarked enemy army and navy.
- A dragon is called from the Divine Realms; Daine heals her.
- Daine calls to the kraken; it helps her defend Pirate's Swoop.
- The kraken destroys enemy forces while the Riders and guard destroy the army.
- Daine finds Skysong, the dragon's kit, after the mother is killed.

Winter/Spring:
- January—Daine turns fourteen.
- The kudarung (winged horses) return to the Copper Islands.
- Dovasary Balitang is born.
- March—A Rider Group disappears.

Summer:
- September—Daine and Numair go to the Long Lake.
- Daine learns of her ability to shape-shift.
- Numair transforms a fellow mage.
- Yolane of Dunlath is captured for plotting treason.
- Maura of Dunlath inherits Dunlath.

Autumn:
- Autumn page training begins:
  - Prince Roald begins training as a page.
  - Cleon of Kennan begins training as a page.
  - Vinson of Genlith begins training as a page.
  - Joren of Stone Mountain begins training as a page.
  - Garvey of Runnerspring begins training as a page.
  - Zahir ibn Alhaz begins training as a page.

Winter/Spring:
- January—Daine turns fifteen.
- April—Edmund of Rosemark is late for page examination. Commanded to repeat all four years, he refuses.

Autumn:
- King Jonathan sends an envoy to Carthak for peace treaties.
- The Graveyard Hag meets Daine.
- Daine learns that her father is the god Weiryn.
- Ozorne kidnaps Daine.
- Daine attacks.
- Ozorne escapes.
- Numair's old teacher Lindhall Reed immigrates to Tortall.
- Prince Kaddar becomes Emperor of Carthak.
- Autumn page training begins:
  - Faleron of King's Reach begins training as a page.
  - Yancen of Irenroha begins training as a page.
  - Balduin of Disart begins training as a page.

Winter:
- December–Midwinter:
  - The barrier between the Realms of the Gods and the Mortals evaporates.

Winter/Spring:
- January—Daine turns sixteen.
- Spring thaw—Daine and Numair help protect the realm as the Immortals War begins.
- April—
  - Nealan of Queenscove begins training as a page.
  - Sir Raoul of Goldenlake is elevated to the peerage, becoming Lord Sir Raoul of Goldenlake and Malorie's Peak.

Summer:
- June—
  - Lord Wyldon rescues the younger princes and princess from hurrocks.

- o Daine and Numair are plucked into the Divine Realms.
- o Daine meets the god Weiryn, the god Gainel, and some animal gods.
- o Daine falls into a spider trap; Numair rescues her.
- o Daine and Numair attend a Dragonmeet.
- o Battle of Port Legann takes place.
- o Daine kills Ozorne.
- o The gods punish Uusoae and decide the fate of the Immortals.
- o Queen Thayet hands command of the Queen's Riders over to Buriram Tourakom.
- o The Immortals War ends.
- o The Mindelan family returns from the Yamani Islands.
- o Eda Bell (the Shang "Wildcat") joins the palace training staff.

Autumn:
- Keladry of Mindelan applies to become a page; Lord Wyldon and King Jonathan agree to put her on probation.
- Kel fights a spidren and decides to train as a page despite the probation.
- Autumn page training begins:
  - o Keladry of Mindelan begins training as a page, sponsored by Neal.
  - o Merric of Hollyrose begins training as a page, sponsored by Faleron.
  - o Seaver of Tasride begins training as a page, sponsored by Prince Roald.
  - o Esmond of Nicoline begins training as a page, sponsored by Cleon.
  - o Quinden of Marti's Hill begins training as a page, sponsored by Zahir.
- Kel receives her first present from her mystery benefactor.

Winter:
- Kel has her first fight with Joren, Vinson, and Zahir.

Winter/Spring:
- Kel has her second fight with Joren and his cronies.
- This winter is described as "the hardest in a decade."
- February—The pages go on an overnight hike.
- The pages have their first all-out brawl (during training).
- March—Lord Wyldon learns of Kel's fear of heights.
- April—Kel has her first page examination.

Summer:
- June—The pages go on a Royal Forest camping trip.
- June—Kel turns eleven.
- Late June—Spidren hunt with the King's Own and Sir Raoul.
- Lord Wyldon allows Kel to continue her training; her probation ends.

Autumn/Winter:
- Princess Kalasin goes to live with the Countess of King's Reach.
- Kel rescues the dog Jump and takes Lalasa Isran as a maid.
- Autumn page training begins:
    - Owen of Jesslaw begins training as a page, sponsored by Prince Roald.
    - Prosper of Tamaran beings training as a page.
    - Teron of Blythdin begins training as a page.
- Kel and Joren have their first conflict of the training year when Kel protects Owen.
- There is a second all-out page brawl in the barn, after training.
- November—Kel begins training Lalasa in self-defense.
- Midwinter—A silent war between Joren's group and Kel's group occurs during the banquet festivities.

Winter/Spring:
- February—Winter camping trip
- April—
    - Joren, Vinson, Cleon, Garvey, Zahir, and Roald all become squires.

- May—
  - ○ Lord Imrah of Legann takes Roald as his squire.
  - ○ Sir Inness of Mindelan takes Cleon as his squire.
  - ○ King Jonathan of Conté takes Zahir as his squire.
  - ○ Sir Paxton of Nond takes Joren as his squire.

Summer/Autumn:
- June camping trip—
  - ○ Kel and company defeat hill men.
  - ○ Kel turns twelve.
- Joren tries to make peace with Kel.
- Autumn page training begins:
  - ○ Warric of Mandash begins training as a page, sponsored by Merric.
  - ○ Iden of Vikison Lake begins training as a page, sponsored by Owen.
- Lord Wyldon begins teaching a Tactics and Strategies class for older pages.
- Lalasa gets her first sewing commission; Kel meets Tianine Plowman.

Winter:
- Midwinter—Uline of Hannalof and Kieran haMinch announce their betrothal.

455 ————————————————————

Winter/Spring:
- March—Vinson attacks Lalasa.
- April—
  - ○ Page examinations are held.
  - ○ Faleron and Yancen become squires.
  - ○ Ragnal of Darroch faints during page examinations.
- Lady Sarugani Balitang dies in a riding accident.

Summer/Autumn/Winter:
- June—
  - ○ The pages take a summer camping trip to fiefs Dunlath, Stone Mountain, and Aili.
  - ○ Kel turns thirteen.

- November—The pages camp overnight in the Royal Forest and do a battle-scenario exercise.
- Southern clans of Scanra unite and elect Maggur Rathhausak to be their war leader.

456 ————————————————

Winter/Spring:
- Queen Thayet commissions a gown from Lalasa.
- April—
  - The Big Exams:
    - Lalasa is kidnapped.
    - Merric, Neal, Esmond, and Quinden become squires.
    - Kel becomes a squire.
  - Kel's secret benefactor buys Peachblossom for her.

Summer:
- June—Kel turns fourteen.
- Sir Raoul takes Kel as a squire.
- Sir Alanna takes Neal as a squire.
- Lalasa opens her own dressmaker's shop.
- Raoul provides Kel with a second mount, Hoshi.
- Kel meets Domitan of Masbolle, sergeant of the King's Own and cousin to Neal.
- The Third Company of the King's Own captures bandits; Kel fights a centaur.
- Kel becomes the adoptive parent of a baby griffin.

Autumn/Winter:
- Kel begins tilting with Raoul.
- The Yamani delegation arrives in Tortall with Princess Shinkokami.
- December—Joren stands trial for paying men to kidnap Lalasa.
  - Kel confronts King Jonathan about legal system injustices.
  - Kel, Raoul, and Thayet press Jon to change a particular law.
- Midwinter—Kel receives her first kiss.

Winter/Spring:

- January—Third Company escorts ambassadors to and from Tyra.
- February—Third Company rids the Bay Cove area of pirates, with help from Baron George Cooper.
- March—Third Company travels south to stay with the Bazhir.
- April—
  - Third Company contains flooding in the Drell River basin region.
  - Owen of Jesslaw becomes a squire.
- May—Third Company returns to the Bazhir and then proceeds to Corus, where the Great Progress has already begun.

Summer/Autumn/Winter:

- June—Kel turns fifteen.
- Kel jousts against Ansil of Groten in a tournament.
- Kel jousts against Sir Voelden of Tirrsmont.
- The griffin's parents come to reclaim their baby, with assistance from Daine.
- Kel tilts with Lord Wyldon at a Fief Blythdin tournament.
- Midwinter—
  - Cleon of Kennan passes his Ordeal of knighthood.
  - Vinson of Genlith survives his Ordeal of knighthood.
  - Joren threatens Kel.
  - Kel learns that Lalasa has been teaching self-defense to common-born girls in the city.
  - Joren of Stone Mountain dies.
  - Lord Buchard of Stone Mountain attacks Kel.
  - Garvey of Runnerspring passes his Ordeal of knighthood.
  - Zahir ibn Alhaz passes his Ordeal of knighthood.
  - Prince Roald of Conté passes his Ordeal of knighthood.
  - Lord Wyldon resigns.

- - Padraig haMinch is chosen as the new training master; Gareth (the Younger) of Naxen takes the interim position.
  - Lord Wyldon takes Owen as his squire.

458 ——————————————————

Winter/Spring/Summer:
- Petranne Balitang is born.
- Landfall, of the Tortallan spy network, begins spying in Hamrkeng, Scanra.
- The Progress stays in Persopolis.
- Bay Cove is struck by an earthquake; Third Company helps refugees and rebuilds the town.
- Spring—At the Blue Harbor tournament, Kel jousts with Wyldon.
- June—
  - The Progress goes to Mindelan.
  - Kel turns sixteen.
- Troops are dispatched to the northern border.
- Roald and Shinkokami take over the Progress (while Jon and Thayet visit troops and nobles).
- Jon and Thayet rejoin the Progress.

Autumn/Winter:
- Lachren of Mindelan (son of Sir Anders) begins training as a page.
- The Progress ends.
- Midwinter—
  - Yancen of Irenroha passes his Ordeal of knighthood.
  - Faleron of King's Reach passes his Ordeal of knighthood.
  - Balduin of Disart passes his Ordeal of knighthood.

459 ——————————————————

Winter/Spring/Summer:
- Elsren of Balitang is born.
- February—Third Company begins resupplying and preparing to head north.

- Nineteen men of the King's Own First Company die in combat.
- April—Third Company begins building a fort along the Scanran border.
- May—Scanrans attack along the coast.
- June—Scanrans attack in the region of Third Company; Kel turns seventeen.
- Mid-August—
  - The Scanran army moves in to take Northwatch.
  - Sir Raoul battles a giant.
  - Kel faces (and defeats) her first killing device.
  - Kel commands a squad.

Autumn/Winter:
- Alan of Pirate's Swoop begins training as a page.
- Mid-September—Encounters with Scanrans drop off.
- Kel and Raoul head back to Corus.
- October—Scanrans attack the village of Goatstrack.
- October/November—Kel helps Shinkokami plan her upcoming wedding and helps Third Company recruit new members.
- Midwinter—
  - Nealan of Queenscove passes his Ordeal of knighthood.
  - Yuki and Neal reveal their mutual affection.
  - Esmond of Nicoline passes his Ordeal of knighthood.
  - Seaver of Tasride passes his Ordeal of knighthood.
  - Quinden of Marti's Hill passes his Ordeal of knighthood.
  - Merric of Hollyrose passes his Ordeal of knighthood.
  - Keladry of Mindelan passes her Ordeal of knighthood.
  - At her knighting ceremony, Kel is given a shield with a distaff border, the first in over 100 years.
  - Alanna gives Kel a sword.

Spring:

- March—
  - ○ Scanra has a new king; Maggur Rathhausak unites the clans under his rule.
  - ○ Kel goes into the Chamber of the Ordeal a second time.
  - ○ Roald and Shinkokami postpone their wedding.
  - ○ The Tortallan army mobilizes.
  - ○ Kel finds Tobeis Boon, an indentured servant.
- April—Cleon returns home.
- Lord Wyldon gives Kel refugee-camp command; Neal and Merric are to serve under her.
- Kel helps soldiers and convicts continue building the camp and names it Haven.
- Numair brings refugees to Haven.
- War is declared between Tortall and Scanra.
- Scanrans attack Haven with killing devices.
- Tirrsmont refugees come to Haven.
- Anak's Eyrie refugees arrive; the Scanrans attack.
- Fort Giantkiller falls.
- May—Minor skirmishes continue with the Scanrans.

Summer:

- May/June—
  - ○ Scanrans attack Haven while Kel is reporting at Fort Mastiff.
  - ○ Lord Wyldon gives Kel orders to bring her troops to Fort Mastiff; Kel decides to rescue the hostages.
  - ○ Raoul secretly sends Dom's squad to track (and help) Kel.
  - ○ Tobe and Owen sneak out to help Kel.
  - ○ Neal sets out with a "rescue party."
  - ○ Kel and company rescue the adult refugees; Kel sends them back with Merric, Seaver, and Esmond, and presses on to find the children.

- o Fanche and Saefas join the group.
- o A child seer, Irnai, dubs Kel the Protector of the Small.
- o Kel and her men rescue the captives with the help of villagers.
- o Kel battles Stenmun.
- o Kel battles Blayce.
- o Kel and company return to Tortall with the abducted children and refugees.
- o Wyldon gives Kel her next command: to build a new refugee camp, to be called New Haven.
- o Kel turns eighteen.

Late Summer/Autumn:
- August-ish—Daine becomes pregnant and can no longer function completely as a spy/wildmage (her child is a shape-shifter in the womb).
- Prince Roald and Princess Shinkokami marry.
- Buri gives up command of the Queen's Riders to Evin Larse.
- September—Kel and Neal return to Steadfast for Raoul and Buri's wedding.
- Irnai foresees that Neal's future daughter will try for knighthood and that his future is littered with surprises.

461 ————————————————

- Prior to February 461, Princess Kalasin has married Emperor Kaddar of Carthak.
- March—Aly returns from a month in Corus with Myles and Eleni.
- April—Aly and Alanna fight over Aly's desire to do field work in the spy organization.
- Aly sets sail for Port Legann; she's captured by pirates and taken as a slave.
- In Rajmuat (capital of the Copper Isles), Aly is sold into the Balitang family service.
- Prince Bronau informs the Balitang family that they have lost favor with King Oron and are being forced into exile.

- The trickster god Kyprioth poses as Mithros in order to convince Duke Mequen and Duchess Winnamine to keep Aly with their family during their exile.
- Aly makes a bet with Kyprioth: she agrees to keep the Balitang children safe through the autumn equinox. If she does this, he will send her back to Tortall and convince her father to let her be a field agent.
- The Balitang party roots out bandits en route to their new home; Sarai and Dove prevent their execution, suggesting a blood oath of fealty instead.
- Kyprioth informs Aly that she will learn the crow language; she is taught primarily by a crow named Nawat. Kyprioth reveals that the crows also have a wager with him.
- Aly discovers that a spy is watching the Crown.
- May—Daine gives birth to her daughter, Sarralyn.
- Frasrlund, on the Tortallan-Scanran border, has been under siege; it reaches a stalemate, each nation occupying a side of the river.
- Jon lets it slip to Alanna that Aly is missing.
- Nawat takes on human form in order to assist Aly.
- Prince Bronau visits Tanair Castle.
- Aly is revealed to the four raka protectors of Sarai and Dove Balitang as Kyprioth's chosen.
- The Balitangs are informed (by Aly) of Prince Bronau's risky situation.
- Junai Dodeka is chosen to be Aly's guard.
- Bronau and the Balitang group go to the village of Pohan; Aly tries to find the local mage.
- June 22—Midsummer's Day—Daine and Numair's daughter has her naming ceremony.
- June/July—
  - Assassins come to Tanair Castle.
  - The duchess allows Sarai and Dove to continue their weapons training, and takes it up herself.
- Bronau proposes to Sarai.

- King Oron dies soon after declaring Prince Hazarin as his successor.
- Prince Bronau leaves for Hazarin's coronation.
- The mage Ochobu Dodeka comes to Tanair Castle to protect Sarugani's heirs.
- Diplomats from Scanra go to Corus to negotiate a peace treaty.
- George leaves for Rajmuat.
- King Hazarin dies; the infant Dunevon is crowned king.
- Prince Bronau tries to kidnap Dunevon and is charged with high treason.
- Aly defends Kyprioth before Mithros and the Goddess.
- Prince Bronau flees to Tanair Castle, where there is fighting.
- The crows take on human form to defend the Balitangs.
- Prince Rubinyan comes to collect his brother; upon learning the course of events, he asks the Balitangs to return to Rajmuat.
- George arrives at Tanair Castle, in search of Aly.

Autumn/Winter:
- Prince Rubinyan tells Duchess Winnamine that there will be no more unnecessary executions.
- Princess Imajane declares full mourning regalia to be "disrespectful to the Black God": only a discreet black armband or black embroidery is appropriate for the mourning of Oron, Hazarin, and Mequen.
- The raka (and Aly) begin seriously planning a rebellion to put Sarai on the throne.
- Dove pieces together the raka conspiracy.

462

Winter:
- The raka continue preparing for revolution in the Copper Isles.
- Tax collectors vanish from their beds, properties are damaged, and nobles and overseers are murdered.
- Sarai refuses to continue her lessons in the sword.

- Aly builds a cadre of trained spies. She earns the nickname "Duani," or "boss lady."

Spring/Summer:
- Aly sends spies to Rajmuat three weeks before the Balitangs' departure from Tanair.
- The Balitang household relocates to Rajmuat, with Mequen's aunt Nuritin.
- Nawat reveals that Kyprioth has made a wager with all of the crows of the Copper Isles, not just the crows of Tanair.
- Dove is let in on the secret of the planned rebellion, and advises the group not to tell Winnamine or Sarai, as Winna would likely make Elsren take the blood oath to leave the way for his sister Sarai to take the crown.
- Aly is questioned by Duke Lohearn Mantawu (Topabaw, head of law enforcement) while the Balitangs go to court to meet the regents for the young king.
- Tkaa, a messenger from Daine, reveals himself at court and gives Aly a message from home.
- Sarai meets Lord Zaimid Hetnim, the (youngest ever) head of the Carthaki Imperial University Healers' Wing (and friend and cousin to Kaddar).
- At Nawat's request, Ulasim sends him along with some other crows to aid distant fighters.
- The Scanran war with Tortall has ended.
- Alan of Pirate's Swoop finds a knight-master.
- Princess Shinkokami awaits the birth of her first child, Lianokami.
- Daine, pregnant with her second child, Rikash, sends darkings to Aly to aid in her spying endeavors. Aly immediately puts them to use.
- The Tortallan spymaster sends funds to the Copper Isles to support the raka rebellion.
- A riot breaks out in the streets—Sarai struggles to help the raka, but Aly and Dove won't permit her. Zaimid heals the raka who are hurt.

- The Dockmarket is blown up magically, and a fire breaks out, destroying ships. All are the workings of Aly and her spies.
- Imajane and Rubinyan hold an eclipse party (reinterpreting standard religion/mythology in order to make it fashionable).
- Aly's spies release political prisoners from the Kanodang fortress. Riots break out in Rajmuat.
- Imajane and Rubinyan offer a marriage contract between Prince Dunevon and Sarai.
- The Graveyard Hag prevents Aly from stopping Sarai from running away with Zaimid.
- Kyprioth lambastes Aly for letting Sarai get away, but she reminds him that Dove is still available and better suited to a queen's work.
- For three days, all the raka businesses and households close down.
- The royal governors of Imahyn and Kerykun are killed.
- Imajane and Rubinyan offer Dove the marriage contract with Dunevon.
- Aly has the army and navy food supplies sabotaged so the regents will press the merchants for food (at lower cost) and make enemies of them.
- King Dunevon, Elsren, and three other boys die in a magical storm, on King Dunevon's birthday.
- Nawat returns from his mission to a joyful reunion with Aly.
- During the week after Dunevon's death, the regent imposes martial law on Rajmuat.
- Winnamine and Nuritin demand to be part of the conspiracy. Duke Nomru and Imgehai Qeshi join in as well.
- Tortall and Carthak put the Copper Isles under a trading ban until the king's murderer is found. Tyra contemplates this action as well.
- August—A riot breaks out in Rittevon Square when assassins try to kill Dove.
  - As the riot in Rittevon Square continues, Aly and the raka sneak into the palace.

- ○ Dove circles above the combat on the kudurung stallion, as a symbol for those who fight in her name.
- ○ There are a great number of casualties.
- By the end of August, only the islands of Ikang and parts of Malubesang and Lombyn resist Dove's rule.
- Kyprioth regains his throne as god of the Copper Isles (and Mithros and the Goddess are looking for their shields, which he has hidden).

Autumn/Winter:

- September—Dove requests that Aly stay on as her spymaster.
- Winnamine and Dove receive a letter from Sarai. She is married, pregnant, and planning to visit as soon as she's able. She plans to name her child Mequen if it's a boy.
- Aly tells Dove, Chenaol, Fesgao, and Winnamine the truth about her origins.
- October—Foreign delegations arrive in the Copper Isles for the official "Season," in preparation for Dove's Midwinter coronation.
- December—The day after the last day of Midwinter, Dove is crowned queen of the Copper Isles.

463 ——————————————————————

- Alan comes to the Copper Isles to bring word that the delegation should return to Tortall.
- Aly marries Nawat.
- April—The Tortallan delegation prepares to head home.
- Aly gives birth to triplets, Ochobai, Ulasu, and Junim.
- Owen of Jesslaw marries Margarry of Cavall, Lord Wyldon and Lady Vivenne's youngest daughter.

Acknowledgments

Each of us came to this project with different skills, different ideas, and different opinions. But there is one thing we all absolutely agree on: we wouldn't be sharing this finished guide with you if not for the work and support of a lot of different people.

All love and thanks are due to Julie, who saved us (a lot) when she pulled together our scattered project as it collapsed, and made it real; and also to Tim, who contributed the original spy teaching manual, giving us our final direction; Lisa, co-writer Megan, and Judy Gerjuoy and her husband, Tero. Thanks are also, obviously, due to Tammy, who created the universe and let us play in it. Mallory Loehr, who started the whole mess and convinced us we could do it, and Chelsea Eberly, who revived and revised this book into the form you're reading now. She encouraged us when we needed it most. Without her, the *Spy's Guide* would have died on the vine.

This book would not be as rich or as beautiful without the design team: Michelle Gengaro, Maria Middleton, Jason Zamajtuk, and Regina Flath. A special thanks to Eva Widermann for the glorious art and to Isidre Mones for the careful mapping.

Thanks also to Raquel Starace and her mom, Gloria; our friends Bruce and Kathy Coville; Tim's brother Craig, who measured distances, and his mother, who provided both emotional and material support during the book's long and sometimes painful growth process.

Very little would have been written without Emily Kramer's tomatoes and Matt Cody's illuminating suggestion that writing could be fun. Moral support for this project was provided by Megan's stage combat family on both coasts; Blake Charlton, doctor and dragon-writer; the Madison Square Lunch dancers; and the Berkeley crew, especially Alice, Andy, Eli, Erika, Juliette, Libby, Mikah, and the lovely Sam. And last but in no way least, years and years of thanks are due to Nina Lourie, the other and better half of Megan's brain.

A final thank-you to Farrah Nakhaie, who constantly helped pick Julie up, dust her off, and set her forward again this past year. She couldn't have done it without the help.

About the Authors

TAMORA PIERCE is the #1 *New York Times* bestselling author of over eighteen novels set in the fantasy realm of Tortall. She first captured the imagination of readers with her debut novel, *Alanna: The First Adventure.* Since then, her bestselling and award-winning works have pushed the boundaries of fantasy and young adult novels to introduce readers to a rich world populated by strong, believable heroines. Her books have been translated into many languages, and some are available on audio from Listening Library and Full Cast Audio. In 2013, she won the Margaret A. Edwards Award for her "significant and lasting contribution to young adult literature."

Pierce lives in Syracuse, New York, with her husband, Tim, and their cats, birds, and occasional rescued wildlife. Visit her at TamoraPierce.com and follow her on Twitter at @TamoraPierce.

JULIE HOLDERMAN writes stuff and loves cats. A once-upon-a-time graduate of the Alpha Workshop for Young Writers, she returned ten years later to serve as a staff member. She studied writing and history at Ithaca College and is eyeing an MA in history, in pursuit of a PhD. She works full-time as Tammy's assistant while building her writing portfolio. Her hobbies include long walks through the library and overanalyzing superhero movies. One day she will stop going to school. Maybe. Probably.

TIMOTHY LIEBE is the "Dreaded Spouse-Creature" and IT Guy for fantasy novelist Tamora Pierce, as well as her coauthor on the Marvel Comics *White Tiger* miniseries. He has written for National Public Radio, CNET, USA Network, and Pacifica Network and spent a decade as a consumer-electronics journalist and editor. An Army brat, Tim traveled the U.S. Midwest and Germany as a child. In the early 1980s, he settled in New York, where he and Tammy still live, surrounded by their (at present) eight cats.

MEGAN MESSINGER's work has appeared in *Cicada, Fantasy Magazine,* and *Electric Velocipede,* as well as other publications, and received honorable mentions in Datlow, Link, and Grant's 2007 *Year's Best Fantasy and Horror.* Megan discovered the books of Tamora Pierce, Bruce Coville, and Jane Yolen while home sick from school—clearly the most fortuitous case of chicken pox ever. In the years since, she's been a writing tutor, theater tech, fight choreographer, Web developer, science-fiction blogger, and nanny. She lives with one foot in Tortall, always; these days, the other foot and most of her vital organs are attending medical school in California.

WHEN YOU GAMBLE WITH KINGDOMS,
ALL BETS ARE OFF.

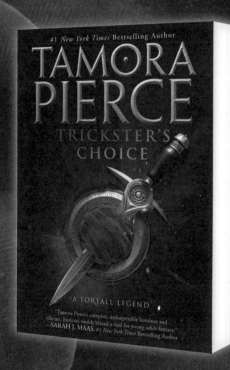

Follow Aly's journey
from slave to spymaster in the
Trickster's Duet.

"Tamora Pierce's complex, unforgettable heroines
and vibrant, intricate worlds blazed a
trail for young adult fantasy."
—SARAH J. MAAS,
#1 *New York Times* bestselling author